The Promise of Frost

Brenda Margriet

COPYRIGHT PAGE

This is a work of fiction. Names, characters, places, and incidents are either the product of the author's imagination or are used fictitiously, and any resemblance to actual persons living or dead, business establishments, events, or locales, is entirely coincidental.

THE PROMISE OF FROST

She tasted of salt and oak and—unexpectedly—cinnamon. Her mouth urged his open, and he almost spilled his drink at the surge of lust and passion that engulfed him when her tongue touched his. Breaking the kiss, he wasted an ounce of very expensive Scotch by shooting it back in one gulp. Luca gazed in astonishment, and then did the same, tossing her glass to the side before launching herself onto his lap and gluing their mouths back together.

The dad part of his brain had a quick moment of *shit, I bet that spilled on the cushions*, before the man part of his brain went *never mind, if you're lucky, there will be even more of a mess to clean up later.*

Luca straddled his hips, her leggings a nearly nonexistent barrier to the heat of her body. He clutched her waist and her sweater was as soft as he'd imagined.

He groaned into her mouth as his fingers slipped under and brushed against the bare, silky skin of her ribs. She pushed against him, her lips devouring his, her breasts squashed with pliable heat against his chest.

In the right circumstances, he would have been all for her zero-to-sixty response. He wasn't sure what he'd been expecting when he'd asked her to stay for a nightcap, but it hadn't been this all-encompassing urge to strip her naked and slam into her until they both found release.

Not with Owen a few steps away and no locked door between his son and the woman he *had* to stop caressing.

In a minute. As soon as he found the willpower.

To the newest members of our family
–

may your first Christmas be only the
start of a lifetime of memories.

CHAPTER ONE

L uca Tannon looked out the window above her kitchen sink and froze.

"Oh, shit," she whispered, and raced outside. "Hold on, little man, I'm coming!"

Silhouetted by the low winter sun, a boy lay stretched out on a branch high up in the tree that grew in her neighbour's yard but overhung the wooden fence separating their spaces. He gave her one quick, half-frightened look, then inched forward determinedly. Just out of his reach, a small black kitten hissed and screeched, staring down at Fergus barking his head off from the ground below.

"Fergus! Quiet!" she commanded.

He ignored her, every scruffy hair on his wiry body vibrating with excitement. His vociferous protest at the alien invasion echoed through the crisp air.

The tree was in the farthest corner, and the snow reached to her knees. Her thick woollen work socks did little to keep out the chill and were already damp, but she hadn't dared stop long enough to put on boots.

Sliding to a halt next to the frantically barking Fergus, she held her arms out. "Don't worry. If you fall, I'll catch you. Can you back up? Just take it easy."

The branch the boy clung to was about three metres above the ground, with nothing in between to break his fall. Luca

1

told herself he wasn't in grave danger, but the consequences could still be nasty if he slipped.

Over Fergus's continuing growls and yaps, the boy said, "I've got to get Waldo. He's scared." He pulled himself forward another inch and the branch bowed.

"Don't go any farther!" Luca said. "It might break."

The boy's movement had set the thinner, more flexible twigs at the end of the limb waggling. The kitten crouched lower, unconcerned by its precarious perch, and rained more invective down on Fergus, who returned it in full force. The cacophony was deafening.

From an invisible source on the other side of the fence, she heard an irritated male voice shout, "Owen Frost! What are you doing?"

"I've got to get Waldo, Dad," the boy said. His small face was pinched and tearful. He wore a red toque and a puffy navy-blue jacket, but his hands were mittenless. "He's stuck in the tree."

"What is he even doing out?" A door banged shut and quick, crunching steps approached. "I told you he needed to stay inside until he got used to us."

"I'm sorry, Dad. I wanted to show him the snow." The boy—Owen—wiped his cheek with one hand, his weight tilting on the branch, and Luca gasped.

"Can't the scolding wait until your son is safe?" she said, raising her voice to be heard over the continuing feline-canine battle.

A man's head and shoulders appeared above the fence. He scowled down at her from dark eyes over-arched by equally dark eyebrows. His head was bare and the icy December breeze that swirled down the neck of Luca's flannel shirt tugged and teased at the brown and silver strands.

"Can't you shut that dog up?" he said. "I can barely hear myself think."

Stung at the contempt in his voice, she said defensively, "He's never seen a cat before. He probably thinks it's a squirrel, and he hates squirrels."

"I don't care if he thinks it's a Grade A steak," Owen's father said. "The cat will never come down with that mutt making such a ruckus."

He was right, of course, but she'd been more concerned about his son than the cat. Snagging Fergus' collar, she dragged him, protesting all the way, into the house. Keeping an eye on the scene in the back corner of her yard, she tugged off her wet socks and slipped her bare feet into a pair of tall, fur-lined winter boots. As she watched, Owen's father put both hands on the top edge of the fence and vaulted lightly into her yard. She was too far away to hear what was being said, but she could see Owen talking, using one hand to gesture in a way that made her breath catch. As she returned to the yard, he sat up, straddling the branch. Taking the last few metres at a run, Luca said, "Careful! Hold on tight now."

The boy's father shot her another darkling look. "He's fine. He shouldn't be up there, but it's just a tree."

"But he might—"

He glared at her and she shut her mouth with a snap.

"He's not going to." Looking back at his son, he held his arms out, much like Luca had before. "Hold onto that branch above you and swing your leg over so you're sitting just like on a chair."

3

Owen did as instructed. "What about Waldo?"

"I'll get him next," his father said. "Now, jump."

Before Luca could draw a breath, Owen slid fearlessly off the branch, landing in his father's arms with a whoop. "Hey, that was fun!" he said, all trace of upset vanished. "Can I do it again?"

"No!" Luca and his father said in unison. With Owen safely on the ground, she offered his father a grin of shared relief. He continued to glare angrily, as if it were all her fault, and her smile faltered.

CALEB FROST KNEW HE was being a jerk, but he hadn't yet recovered from the fright of seeing Owen insecurely balanced several metres off the ground. Now his son was safe, he could admit the branch was thick and sturdy, but until this moment all he'd been able to envision was wood snapping beneath his son's light weight, sending him plummeting to the snow-covered, frozen earth below.

The last thing he'd wanted to do, though, was let Owen know how scared he was. It was easy to see his son had been on the verge of freezing in fear, no thanks to the well-meaning but cosseting actions of Luca Tannon. Speaking and acting calmly and confidently while his son dangled from the limb had taken up all his energy, leaving none for social niceties.

He gripped Owen on the shoulder, feeling how thin and fragile the bones were, and swallowed down the urge to shout. "The next time Waldo climbs a tree," he instructed, "you come and get me. Do *not* try and rescue him yourself."

"Aww, Dad…"

"Promise me, Owen."

His son rolled his eyes. "I promise."

Caleb was keenly aware of Luca watching their exchange. Her gaze flicked back and forth between them but she remained silent. Despite the winter weather, she wore no jacket, just a heavy flannel shirt. A grey ball cap with the words *Apex Transport* stitched in black on the crown covered her short hair, and her worn, grimy jeans were marked on the thigh with what appeared to be grease.

Gritting his teeth, he prepared to do his best to repair the situation. Turning to Luca, he said, "I'm Caleb Frost. This is my son, Owen."

"Luca Tannon," she replied with a sharp lift of her chin.

He didn't bother explaining he knew her name already. The postal delivery person had an irritating habit of leaving her mail in his box. She didn't know that, though, as Caleb had plenty of time to correct the mistake without risking any personal interaction while she was at work. She was always out of the house well before five every morning and didn't return until around three, sometimes later.

It wasn't creepy he knew so much about her, he assured himself. He hadn't searched out the information—he was just naturally observant.

"Thank you for trying to help," he said stiffly. Her green eyes narrowed and he realized how ungrateful that sounded. He was really making a muck of this. Maybe if he'd introduced himself four months ago when he'd moved into the duplex, this wouldn't be so awkward.

Owen stared anxiously up into the tree. "What about Waldo, Dad? He's still up there. I don't think he knows how to get down."

As if responding to his name, the kitten picked his way delicately along the branch toward the trunk of the tree and hopped down with a feline insouciance that Caleb had to admire. "Well, he's figured it out now. Here, go get him." He lifted Owen with two hands under his armpits and swung him over the fence. "Ready?" His son nodded and Caleb let go. Owen vanished, and a moment later he could hear him calling to Waldo.

Luca was staring at Caleb with raised eyebrows. "There's a gate, you know." She jerked a thumb over her shoulder to the gap on the far side of her house. The fence he'd just tossed Owen over was an extension of the wall the two connected homes shared.

He shrugged. "This was faster. But I'll go that way if you don't mind." He'd managed to scramble over the fence when his adrenalin had been pumping, but was pretty sure he'd make a fool of himself if he tried to do it again.

She matched his gesture. "Whatever floats your boat."

Her casual dismissal shouldn't raise the hackles between his shoulders, but it did. It wasn't only his fault they hadn't yet met. She had expressed no interest whatsoever in knowing him, either, offering only a cool *hello neighbour* nod on the rare occasions they'd seen each other.

Which was exactly the way he wanted it, of course. Since the divorce, his focus had been on helping Owen adjust, and that's where it needed to remain.

Snow clung to his jeans and damp seeped through the breathable material of his running shoes. He'd hastily donned the nearest footwear after Luca's dog's frenzied barking had alerted him to Owen's predicament. He had nothing against dogs—well-behaved ones, at least—and he felt a little guilty at his rudeness regarding her pet earlier.

"What's your dog's name?" he said, by way of an olive branch.

"Fergus. Don't worry, I won't let his barking bother you again," Luca said coldly. They'd reached the side gate. "Goodbye."

He'd really made a mess of things, but he couldn't leave Owen and Waldo alone any longer. Look what had happened in the five minutes he'd been on the phone with a client. "Goodbye."

She nodded and turned her back, disappearing around the corner of the house before he'd even opened the gate.

Once out of the yard, he made sure the latch locked securely behind him, not wanting to be responsible for Fergus escaping. A concrete sidewalk led across the front of Luca's house and, as he squished damply along it, he noted the meagre string of Christmas lights framing the front window and the knee-high plastic Santa set on the stoop.

He passed her tiny, bright green compact car and stepped through the metre-wide strip of snow that separated his parking area from hers. His and Owen's half of the duplex was a stark contrast to Luca's.

Well, *stark* was probably the wrong word.

Caleb might have been overcompensating for the fact this was Owen's first Christmas as the child of divorced parents.

Lights edged the gutters, the window, and the railings leading up to the front door. An enormous inflatable snow globe almost blocked the view from the window, but as he climbed the steps, he could still see the gaudily decorated Christmas tree in the front room.

Inside, he removed his soaked shoes and socks and padded barefoot to the kitchen. The laundry room was tucked between it and the back entrance, and he tossed his footwear into the dryer, setting it thumping on a low setting to get the worst of the wet out.

The back door opened and Owen, obviously none the worse for wear, raced in. He trailed a thin, bright red leash, and Waldo followed, a black and white streak as he pounced with ferocious delight on his wriggling victim.

"Take off your boots!" Caleb bellowed before Owen went any farther. His son screeched to a halt, kicked so hard his boots thudded against the wall leaving damp smudges, and sprinted down the hall, the cat in pursuit.

Caleb made sure the exterior door had swung shut behind the playmates and straightened the boots and shoes in the small back entry area. Then he returned to the kitchen, where the bits and pieces of not-yet-started gingerbread houses littered the table. He and Owen had barely begun this Christmas tradition when Caleb had been called away for a quick phone consult with a new, nervous client—and the rest was history.

The disarray contrasted sharply with the neatly organized kitchen, and Caleb felt a twitch between his shoulder blades. "Owen! Come finish your house. I want to get these done before dinner." He glanced at the clock on the stove. It wasn't yet four. Luca must have barely gotten home from work when all the excitement started.

His son skidded around the corner from the hall into the kitchen. "Waldo's using his litter box," he said breathlessly.

"Good." The kitten had only joined the family the past weekend and was proving to be neat and tidy. Caleb didn't agree with pets as Christmas gifts, but could admit his timing on giving in to Owen's persistent wishes might have had something to do with the holiday season.

"Can we make three houses?" Owen knelt on one of the kitchen chairs and reached for a gingerbread wall. "Do we have enough stuff?"

"I think so. Why?" Caleb helped him run a line of icing down the tinfoil he'd wrapped around a stiff cardboard sheet. Together, they placed the wall into it. "Hold this for a bit while I add more icing along the edge."

"I want to give one to the lady next door. She looked kind of scared when she saw me on the branch." His tongue stuck out of the corner of his mouth as he concentrated on holding the wall steady. "I wasn't scared, though. 'Cause I'm a boy."

Mildly shocked yet wholly amused at that chauvinistic statement, Caleb said, "I'm a boy and I was scared. We were both worried you'd fall and get hurt." He felt a twinge of remorse. She'd been protecting his son, and all Caleb had done was snap at her.

"Like I was worried about Waldo?"

"Something like that." They placed the second wall. "So, you want to give her a gingerbread house to apologize?"

"Everybody likes gingerbread houses."

9

"True." It would be a nice gesture, Caleb thought. And maybe it would help Luca forgive him for his own boorish behaviour, as well as the fright his son had given her. "Okay, let's do that. We'll have to make it extra special."

CHAPTER TWO

Luca pulled into her driveway after work the next day and stared at the gaily wrapped present sitting on the front stoop next to her vaguely pathetic Santa.

December dusk fell by midafternoon in northern British Columbia, and the outside light she'd left on to welcome her home sparked glints from the shiny silver wrapping. The timer she'd set had also illuminated the string of lights around her front window, but her side of the duplex paled in comparison to the Frosts'. Next year she'd have to do better.

Her Grinchiness was one more thing to lay at Trent's door.

Shoving aside the unwelcome thoughts of her ex, she gathered her lunch kit and thermos mug from the passenger seat and squeezed out of her tiny car. The guys at work always teased her about it, laughing that it would fit in the cab of her tractor-trailer unit. They were right, but she didn't need anything bigger to boot around town in. Why not drive something she could practically park in her pocket and ran for several weeks on one tank of gas?

As she neared the package, her curiosity grew. Taped to the box was a computer printed message that read *To Ms. Tannon. THIS SIDE UP. Open here.* An arrow pointed to a tab sticking out from the top edge.

She opened the door and put her kit and mug on the top shelf of the closet before bending to undo her heavy, steel-toed work boots. Shaking them off, she shrugged out of her jacket and the reflective safety vest she wore over it. Only then did she step back outside to retrieve the package. Kicking the door shut, she headed to the kitchen, placed the box on the counter, and went to release Fergus from his pen by the back door where he spent his time when she wasn't home.

He greeted her with friendly barks, his dust mop tail wagging vigorously. She gave him his expected scrub around the ears in greeting and then left him loose so he could reconnoiter the yard and do his business.

In the kitchen once more, she studied the box, knowing if she opened it, she'd solve the mystery of what was in it, but savouring the anticipation a while longer. She was *that person* on birthdays and Christmases—the one that took forever to open her gifts. Her parents always laughed indulgently and said she'd been that way all her life, but it drove her siblings and Trent mad. *Had* driven Trent mad. What did and didn't irritate him was no longer her concern, thank goodness.

She gripped the small tab as directed and pulled.

The front of the box lowered, rather like the ramp on the trailers of the transport trucks she drove, revealing a gaudily decorated gingerbread house.

Smiling widely, but more mystified than ever, she worked her fingertips under the tinfoil base and slid it forward. The walls were crooked and the chimney leaned at a gravity-defying angle. Every inch on one side of the roof was covered in candy in a random pattern, while on the other side red and green Smarties alternated in tidy rows. Mini candy canes drunkenly lined a neat path made from dark chocolate shavings.

A scrape and whine at the back door let her know Fergus was ready to come in. She opened it and he bounded by, heading straight for the wicker basket in the living room where his toys were kept. A rhythmic squeaking began, and she knew he had settled onto the couch with his favourite squishy.

Nothing about the gingerbread house revealed who had sent it. Peering inside the box again, she discovered an envelope stuck to the side. She peeled it off and opened it. It contained two short notes, each in a different handwriting. The letters of the first were scrawly and unformed, the words filling the entire page. She read:

Dear Ms. Tannon,

I am sorry I scared you when I was in the tree. I wasn't scared but my dad says sometimes grownups get scared for kids even when the kids are okay. I hope you aren't mad at me.

Sincerely, Owen Frost

The second was written in tiny, cramped writing that was nevertheless clearly legible. It reminded her of the text she'd seen on blueprints and engineering schematics.

Ms. Tannon,

Please accept this small gift as an apology for my behaviour yesterday. I didn't want Owen to know how badly he'd frightened me and took it out on you and

Fergus. I hope it will not affect our neighbourly relationship.

Sincerely, Caleb Frost

Despite the stilted tone, the father's words appeared as refreshingly honest as the son's, and she couldn't help smiling. *Caleb Frost.* She probably should have introduced herself much sooner—they'd shared a wall for months, after all—but she'd been strictly off men at the time, still getting over Trent.

She gritted her teeth. Thinking about him three times since she'd arrived home was three times more than he deserved. Not all men were jerks and, despite her first impressions of Caleb, she believed his explanation of his actions. Which made him one of the not-jerks.

Maybe it was time to ease up on her rule.

"OKAY, NEXT WORD." CALEB took his attention from the peanut butter and jam sandwich he was making to look at the list Owen had given him. "Family."

Tongue poking out between his teeth, Owen scrawled the word into his exercise book. Thursdays were Spelling Test Day in his Grade 3 classroom, which meant Wednesdays Caleb helped him study, on the evenings Owen wasn't with his mother.

"Done," Owen said.

"The next word is au—" Caleb was cut off by a rapid, knocking tattoo.

"I'll get it!" Owen shouted, thrilled as always to put off homework as long as possible. He rocketed off his chair and dashed to the door, startling Waldo from his nap on the cat tree next to the living room window. The kitten darted into one of the enclosed spaces and peered out suspiciously.

"Check who it is, first!" Caleb called. He pressed the top slice of bread onto the sandwich and wiped his hands on a dishcloth before following his son at a more sedate pace.

"It's Ms. Tannon." Owen looked over his shoulder and, at Caleb's nod, unlocked and opened the door. Luca stood on the stoop, wearing a padded jacket and furry boots. Her head was bare today, the short, choppy strands a rich dark brown glowing warmly in the beams from the porch light.

"Hi there, Owen," she said cheerfully. "I wanted to thank you and your dad for the lovely gingerbread house and the notes. That was very thoughtful."

"It was my idea," Owen said, throwing his father under the bus without compunction. "Though Dad did help me spell some of the words."

"He did a fine job. They were nearly all right."

Caleb choked and then caught the gleam in Luca's eyes. "I did my best," he said drily, and the gleam brightened.

"Dad and I shared the decorating," Owen said. "Which roof did you like better?"

"I liked both sides equally," Luca said diplomatically.

Owen's grin dimmed. "But Dad didn't put nearly as many candies on his. And only two colours."

She recovered without losing a beat. "Well, I didn't want to hurt your dad's feelings, but"—she leaned down and whispered into Owen's ear, loud enough for Caleb to hear—"*your* side is really my favourite. Thank you for all the candies."

His son grinned and gave him a smug look.

"What do you say, Owen?" Caleb said.

"You're welcome," he said obediently. "I'm glad you like it."

Luca straightened and met Caleb's gaze, lifting her chin minutely while raising her eyebrows in an unmistakable signal.

"Your sandwich is ready," Caleb said to Owen. "Why don't you go have your snack and I'll come help with the rest of your homework in a minute. Say goodbye to Ms. Tannon."

"Goodbye, Ms. Tannon." Owen sighed and dragged his feet down the hallway.

"Call me Luca," she called after him. "Talk to you later, little man."

Owen grinned at her over his shoulder and disappeared into the kitchen. Waldo jumped down from his perch and followed.

Luca jerked her head and backed away from the opening. The temperature was mild for a December day, so Caleb didn't bother getting a coat, just slipped his feet into a handy pair of shoes and followed her out, shutting the door behind him.

She wasted no time. "I think we got off on the wrong foot yesterday," she said. "Thank you for your apology, and please accept mine. I didn't mean to make things worse."

He lifted one shoulder awkwardly. "No, you were just trying to help. I may have overreacted."

"You were worried about Owen. I get that. I wanted to let you know it's all good." She wiped her palms together, as if dusting off the past. "Well, I should go. Fergus needs a walk." She took a small step back, the heel of her boot near the top edge of the stoop, and he instinctively put out his hand, though she was in no danger of tumbling down the steps.

Luca must have interpreted his gesture as a handshake. She clasped his fingers, her grip strong, warm, and slightly rough. The shock of her touch zipped up his arm and directly to his groin.

For a moment, he could do nothing but stand frozen, linked skin to skin, palm to palm.

Her green eyes widened and she dropped his hand abruptly. "Thanks again for the gingerbread house. And the notes. See you around." She hurried down the steps and disappeared inside her house.

He stood on the stoop a little longer. The surge of sexual attraction was surprising—and unwelcome. While things were well and truly over with his ex-wife, he had no interest in a new relationship of any sort. Owen had struggled with his parents' separation, and Caleb had vowed to put his son's well-being ahead of everything else.

And *certainly* ahead of getting to know his new neighbour, no matter how appealing she might be.

CHAPTER THREE

When Luca first met Trent, she'd loved his ambition, his drive, his focus on success. It had been a true case of opposites attract. He had a Master's in Finance—she'd dropped out of college after the first semester. His preferred meal was four courses with the appropriate wine pairings—hers, pizza, and beer. He thrived on networking with the influential people in their town—she would rather stay home watching sports on television.

Nervous about attending the corporate events and cocktail parties he frequented, she had gladly accepted his advice on her clothes, her makeup, her *performance*. At first, the act had been necessary only when they were in public, but slowly it had bled over until she was no longer herself even when they were alone.

It had taken her years to realize she was only an accessory in Trent's never-ending search for success. Years of coming second, third, or even fourth on his list of priorities. Years of pushing aside her own wants and needs for his.

Once she *had* realized, she'd acted, and in the months since she'd left him, she'd found a measure of contentment and happiness, and had learned to enjoy being alone, other than for Fergus and her family. She'd been perfectly happy with her mechanical boyfriends and had had no desire to get back out into the dating world.

But the brief contact she and Caleb had shared that afternoon had sparked a yearning for human touch.

Fergus sighed and rested his chin on her thigh. She smoothed one silky ear—the only sleek fur on his wiry, scruffy body. They were in their favourite spot, stretched out on the couch, enjoying a quiet evening not really watching the hockey game playing on her TV. She'd taken him for a long walk after her visit to Owen and Caleb, and then she'd fed them dinner. It was just after seven, and she'd be going to bed soon since she had to be up at four-thirty, but for now she could relax.

If only she could stop thinking about that handshake.

She didn't believe in love at first sight. *Lust*, however—that was different. *Lust* at first sight was perfectly reasonable since it was just the right combination of pheromones and hormones and whatever-other-mones at the right time and in the right place.

She'd never seen a woman at the house next door, and the surreptitious glance she'd taken at Caleb's left hand hadn't revealed a wedding band. Neither of which meant she was free to act on any of the urges she was currently suppressing. Maybe he never wore a ring. Maybe his wife was in the army and stationed overseas. Maybe he was gay and was separated from his partner.

She really hoped it wasn't the last, given the surge of attraction she'd felt at the clasp of his palm.

Still, she had to find out more before taking another step.

THE PROMISE OF FROST

CALEB READ THE NOTE again, still not entirely sure how to react.

Dear Caleb,

If you don't ask, you don't get, so here's me asking.

Question A: Are you currently married? If yes, please skip to end. If no, continue to Question B.

Question B: Are you interested in exploring whatever it was we felt when we shook hands? (That is, if you felt it, too. I think you did, but I've been wrong before. Not often, but it has happened LOL.) If no, please skip to end. If yes, continue to Question C.

Question C: Are you available Saturday night at eight o'clock?

Thanks again for the gingerbread house.

In neighbourliness,

Luca

He'd found the envelope containing it tucked in with his other mail this morning, though its lack of stamp had alerted him to the fact it had been hand delivered.

It was the oddest, most intriguing letter he'd ever read.

For one, he'd never been asked out on a date by a woman before. For another, the whole tone was so light and breezy, he could easily dismiss it as a joke.

That he didn't *want* to dismiss it unsettled him.

He placed it precisely in a corner of his desk and leaned toward his keyboard with a determined air, resolving to ignore it. Whether he would do so until he achieved progress on coding the app for the new client he'd signed a couple weeks ago, or for good, he didn't specify, even to himself.

The duplex he'd bought several months after his divorce only had two bedrooms, but the basement had enough space for the treadmill he used when the weather was too miserable for running outside as well as a walled off area that sufficed for his home office. Windows set partially below ground level and protected by metal wells provided dim daylight but didn't cause troublesome reflections on his various computer monitors. The two trestle tables he used as desks fit neatly in the corners, and he'd strapped all the cables underneath to hide their snaking confusion. The bare walls were unfinished drywall and the floor boasted only a thin covering of industrial grade carpet but, as he didn't bring clients to his home, the rather tatty decor didn't matter. Maybe someday he'd need a real office. For now he was fine where he was.

Mentally gritting his teeth, he managed to put in a solid chunk of work before the ache in his back and shoulders grew too insistent. Gone were the days when eight hours hunched over a keyboard hadn't made his spine seize and his neck stiffen. He stood, did a few easy stretches, and then picked up his coffee cup and Luca's letter and trudged up the stairs. The basement access opened into the kitchen, and for a moment he stood still, blinking at the sunshine blaring in through the window. Bright blue skies in December usually meant bitter temperatures, but he'd take the cold and sun of northern

British Columbia over than the gloomy skies and incessant rain of the Lower Mainland any day.

Tossing the dregs of his coffee into the sink, he refilled his water bottle and leaned a hip against the counter as he drank.

And thought about Luca's letter, lying face up on the counter beside him.

Owen would be starting his next turn with his mother on Saturday. As a nurse at the local hospital, Teri worked twelve-hour shifts—two days, followed by two nights, followed by a few days off, then two nights and two days, and so on and so on. It meant their custody-sharing of Owen wasn't the usual one-week-with-Mom, one-week-with-Dad, rotation. One of the few things they *hadn't* argued about during their divorce proceedings was the fact that their son would not be raised by caregivers. In order to have the flexibility necessary to balance Teri's shift work, Caleb had left his job at a local computer firm and become a freelance programmer.

All of which was the long way of saying he was available Saturday night at eight o'clock. If he wanted to be.

He was surprised to realize he *did* want to be.

It had been months since he'd had the time or the inclination to consider dating. Owen had had a very difficult time accepting his parents' divorce, suffering nightmares and separation anxiety. When Owen was with Caleb, his focus was on helping his son understand nothing was his fault and providing the attention he needed to get past this shock to his life. Then, when Owen was with Teri, Caleb concentrated on growing his business. Luckily, his old bosses had tossed a few jobs his way and the change had been relatively painless, but he couldn't take that for granted. Freelancing meant a less stable source of income, and he was putting in more hours now than he had when he'd been an employee to make sure that early success didn't falter.

Waldo strolled in and stropped himself on Caleb's ankles, but when he was ignored, he stalked back out, tail stiff with disgust, and disappeared.

Would it be fair to Luca to accept her invitation? Since she'd mentioned the zing of sexual attraction in her letter, he couldn't ignore the possibility she wanted to explore more than just a friendship. His marriage had left wounds that weren't quite healed, and he knew he wasn't ready for anything serious yet—maybe never would be. But the flipside of commitment was a string a short-term, casual dates, and there was no way he could expose Owen to the uncertainty of those kinds of relationships.

Caleb shook his head, disgusted with himself. He had a dangerous habit of looking so far into the future that it paralyzed him in the present. One date with Luca was simply that—one date. She intrigued him, and he couldn't deny she was right about the tension that tugged between them.

He would go. But he wouldn't mention it to Owen.

LUCA DIDN'T *expect* to find a reply from Caleb waiting for her when she arrived home that afternoon.

Hoped for, but didn't *expect*.

Which was why, when there was nothing in her mailbox except flyers and an unwanted increase-your-limit-now notice from her credit card company, she told herself she wasn't disappointed. Caleb didn't strike her as the spontaneous type. He probably needed to think about her invitation carefully, weigh all the pros and cons, maybe even sleep on it overnight.

Unless he'd answered *yes* to Question A, of course. If he was married, her plans were stalled before she even put the key in the ignition.

Her afterwork routine always involved a walk with Fergus. She was clipping the leash to his halter when a knock sounded at the front door.

The dog danced impatiently around her feet, yipping with excitement. "Hush," she said. "We'll get going in a minute."

Her heart gave a hard thump when she saw Caleb standing on the stoop. "Hi, there," she said, determined to be casual. No matter what his answer, they were still going to be neighbours. No need to make things more awkward than they had to be.

Fergus barked a greeting, prancing on his hind legs. She shortened his leash to prevent him from jumping on Caleb. Her pet really needed to work on his manners.

"Hi," Caleb said, eyeing Fergus but refraining from comment. "Did I catch you on your way out?"

"Just going for a walk." The sun was almost gone, but their winter excursions were often in darkness given the shortness of the days. The delay didn't matter. She'd rather know his decision now than wait until later.

He nodded and shifted his weight, his breath making clouds in the brisk air.

She stepped back, dragging Fergus with her. He'd stopped barking but still regarded Caleb like a long-lost friend, panting excitedly. "Come on in. It's cold out there." He wore only a light jacket and running shoes.

He remained where he was. "I won't keep you long. I wanted to let you know I got your letter. My answers are *no* to Question A. And *yes* to Questions B and C."

She blinked. "Oh. Okay. Good."

"So, I'll see you Saturday? At eight?"

A grin spread across her face as her brain caught up with her ears. "Yes, Saturday at eight. Wear warm clothing." She dipped her chin to acknowledge his current outfit. "Winter boots. Ski pants if you've got them. All the fixin's."

His expression morphed from nervous to faintly horrified. "Where are you taking me?"

"To the stars."

CHAPTER FOUR

Caleb folded himself into the passenger seat of Luca's ridiculously tiny car. He wasn't an extra tall man—thank goodness, given his current cramped situation. Anyone more than six feet would have to stick their legs out the window to fit.

Even before squeezing onto the seat, he'd felt bloated and awkward, dressed in his puffy parka, insulated pants, and tall boots. Luca wore a similar outfit, and the sleeves of their coats brushed each other in the close confines. While he gave an impression of the Pillsbury Dough Boy, though, Luca looked cozy and comfortable and completely at home in her winter gear.

"Are you sure you wouldn't rather take my car?" he asked as she started the engine, which whined like a lawnmower on helium.

"Don't worry, we're not going far. Just to a friend's place."

She had refused to tell him anything more about her plans. He was pretty sure she didn't have a rocket ship hiding in a farmer's silo, so *to the stars* couldn't be a literal description of their destination. Given her wardrobe instructions, he assumed she meant something innocuous like sitting around a campfire and gazing at the night sky.

Still, he couldn't help but feel a little nervous.

Eight o'clock on a December evening might as well have been midnight. Colourful twinkling lights on homes and businesses did their best to overcome the dark, and more elaborate Christmas displays glowed in defiance of the gloom. But in less than ten minutes, they left the city streets behind. Traffic grew scarce as they travelled the highway leading north, the headlights of Luca's car stabbing through the dark like sword thrusts. Only occasionally did the great swathes of blackness on either side sparkle with holiday lights, the distant indication of rural homes and farm buildings.

Luca had chosen an all-Christmas playlist on her phone and seemed content to focus on driving, occasionally singing along under her breath. Caleb found the lack of conversation restful. He shifted in his seat, searching for a slightly more comfortable position, and she glanced over at him, but only smiled before directing her gaze forward once more.

As time went on, he began wondering exactly what her concept of *not far* was. About half an hour after passing the city boundary, she slowed and took a turn to the left, crossing the railroad track that was currently running parallel to the highway before regaining speed along a narrow curving road that ran through a forest of tall trees. A small sign flashed by.

"Summit Lake?" he said, raising his voice above a country version of *Baby, It's Cold Outside*.

"Yes. Almost there."

A minute later she took another left, this time down a private drive. Her car bumped and shuddered over the snow-rutted, tree-lined track before popping out into a wide-open space. A small cabin appeared directly ahead with an outbuilding to his right. Snow had been plowed into piles at the edges, leaving the centre clear enough that even Luca's Tonka Toy could manoeuvre easily.

She parked next to the outbuilding. "Here we are."

"Uh-huh." He peered through the windshield. Other than a security light over the door of the cabin, and another on a pole near the outbuilding that illuminated the parking area, there were no signs of life. "Where exactly is *here?*"

"A friend of mine's cabin."

"It doesn't look like she's expecting visitors."

She laughed. "He's not here. Don't worry, though, I have permission. Come on."

She opened her door and he followed suit. The car was so low to the ground it might have been easier to roll out, given his ungainly attire, but he struggled to his feet, hoping Luca wasn't paying attention to his graceless exit.

The snow squeaked as they trod toward the double doors of the shed. Luca took a key from her pocket, inserted it into the padlock securing the entrance, and unfastened it. Pulling one side wide, she gestured for him to do the same with the other and he complied.

The space was full of the random tools and equipment he'd expect to see in a shed, including a ride-on lawnmower, shovels, deflated water toys, buckets, deck chairs, and a chainsaw. Directly before them was a large, tarpaulin-covered bulk. Luca whipped off the covering and revealed a shiny gleaming monster of a snowmobile.

"READY FOR A RIDE?" Luca said, rather enjoying the squeamish look on Caleb's face.

"I've never been on a snowmobile before." He studied the machine like it might bite.

"Really? Where did you grow up?" Straddling the seat of the sled, she reached into her pocket to retrieve the key her buddy had given her at work the day before and slid it into the ignition.

"Vancouver." He continued to watch her warily.

She tilted her head to one side. "A city boy," she teased. "When did you move to Prince George?"

"Right after university. I couldn't find work down south, so started applying all over the province. I figured I'd come for a couple years, get some experience, then go back." He shrugged. "That was twenty years ago."

"And in all that time no one's ever taken you snowmobiling?"

"I'm more of an indoor kind of guy," he said with a self-deprecating quirk of his mouth.

"Let me fire her up," she said, "and we'll get her outside."

A few minutes later the sled was idling nicely, the shed was once again locked, and Luca had strapped the insulated bag she'd packed with drinks and snacks onto the back. Taking off her toque and shoving it in her pocket, she secured the strap of her borrowed helmet under her chin and straddled the seat, sliding forward so her knees were tucked up against the dash. She held out a second helmet to Caleb. "Hop on."

He didn't move from his stance a few steps away. "Will you revoke my man card if I admit this makes me nervous? I like my transportation to have a little more"—he waggled his gloved hands in a gesture that encompassed her and the sled—"well, more. A roof. Doors."

"We're not going far, we're not going fast, and I promise to be careful."

Squaring his shoulders as if preparing for a firing squad, he accepted the helmet and mimicked her actions with his toque before buckling it on. "The last time you said we weren't going far, we drove for an hour," he muttered, but he swung his leg over the seat without further demur. His weight settled behind her with a gap between their bodies. She twisted the throttle gently and set the sled in motion.

The instant it powered forward, Caleb's arms wrapped around her waist and squeezed. His thighs bracketed hers and, even through the thick layers of their combined clothing, she was aware of his heat and strength.

Maybe too much strength.

"You might want to let me breathe," she shouted over the noise of the engine. "We're perfectly safe."

The band around her belly eased as she guided the sled down the modest slope past the cabin. She knew the moment Caleb realized she was taking him onto the surface of the lake when his grip tightened painfully again.

"We're going out on the ice?" His voice was loud in her ear. And a higher register than normal.

"It's okay. I promise. Lots of machines have been out here already. Look." She used one mittened hand to point ahead of them. The headlight showed the corrugated tracks of other sleds, and she felt Caleb's embrace ease once more.

Increasing her speed gradually, they roared along the trail. Wind whipped her cheeks and made her eyes water, and she kicked it up another notch with a sense of gleeful freedom.

If she'd been alone, she might have dipsied and doodled her way across the lake, tested the power and manoeuverability of the sled with tight corners and figure-eights. In deference to the newbie behind her, she kept to the straight and narrow.

Summit Lake was a squashed crescent shape with an irregular shoreline and various arms and islands. From their starting point, heading due west took them along the lower part of the crescent, away from the cabins clustered on the shores nearest the highway. By the time she reached her destination, a secluded bay, there wasn't an artificial light in sight. She pulled to a stop and turned off the engine. Only the whisper of a slight breeze brushing the snow-covered ice filled the silence left behind.

Luca took off her helmet and tugged on her toque. "Look," she said, pointing at the sky.

THOUGH HIS ARMS WERE still wrapped around Luca's waist, Caleb was no longer nervous. Her competence in controlling the powerful machine had been obvious within moments, and he'd actually enjoyed their transit across the wintry expanse. In fact, he could have let her go long before, except it had seemed natural to continue holding her.

It had been a long time since he'd hugged a woman unrelated by blood or marriage. He couldn't say the spark sizzling through his nerves was a surprise, given his reaction to her touch the other day, but it made him wary. Liking Luca was one thing. Lusting after her something else entirely.

Reluctantly releasing her, he took off his helmet and looked where she'd pointed.

And gasped.

The night sky was washed in glittering lights, countless millions of them. This wasn't the faded, lacklustre view he was used to. He suddenly understood the definition of the word *cosmos*.

"I know what you mean," Luca said, as if he'd actually spoken his wonder. "If we're really lucky, we might see shooting stars. The Geminids don't peak for a couple nights yet, but you never know."

"The Geminids?" Without taking his eyes from the vast vista before him, he pulled on his toque. Even the enthralling sight wasn't enough to distract him from the bitter wind nipping at his ears.

"A meteor shower. Happens every December around this time. It is supposed to be an especially good year, as it coincides with the new moon. No extra light to distract from them."

The sky was huge above the wide sweep of frozen water. Luca tilted her chin up and, given her position in front of him, her head almost rested on his shoulder. Realizing he could use the pack strapped behind him as a support, he leaned back. After a short, silent battle between his wants and his worries, he put his hands on her shoulders and drew her towards him. It would be easier for her to look up, he told himself. It had nothing to do with wanting to feel her nestled against him.

At first, she resisted, but then she settled back with a soft sigh. As they stared at the constellations sparkling above, the clouds of their breath merged and mingled.

Between one blink and the next, a streak of light slashed from left to right.

"There," Luca said, sitting upright. A rush of cold air filled the space she left behind. "Did you see it?"

"I did." Despite his intention to keep Owen and Luca in two separate spheres of his life, he had a sudden wish his son was with them, sharing this moment. "My first shooting star."

She twisted her torso to look at him over her shoulder. The only light was what reflected off the snow, and all colour was leeched from her skin, hair, and eyes. But her grin was as bright as the dying meteor he'd just seen.

"You have to make a wish," she said. "It's tradition."

"You don't believe in that sort of stuff, do you?"

"There's believing and then there's *believing*," she said. "Like Santa Claus. You can believe, even though you know it's Mom and Dad."

The urge to kiss her was so strong and so sudden he jerked back. It had been a mistake, letting down his guard, enjoying the feel of her in his arms. It made him want what he wasn't ready for. "I'm not making a wish."

Wishes were dangerous. Wishes were trouble. Wishes were for children, not grown adults with responsibilities and obligations.

Her grin faded, the gleam of her teeth disappearing. "Your loss," she said lightly. "I brought snacks and drinks. Let's dig those out before we get too cold and need to head back."

CHAPTER FIVE

S unday morning, Luca took Fergus for an especially long hike to apologize for not bringing him with her and Caleb. Though she didn't own her own snowmobile, she had enough friends and family with the machines that Fergus had spent plenty of time around them, and he would have loved a run out on the frozen lake. But she didn't normally take him along on dates, so had left him at home with a consoling pat and a new chew toy.

She had plenty to chew on herself as she trudged the winding paths of one of their favourite wilderness trail systems. Fergus dashed in and out of the bushes, happily chasing invisible scents but never straying far. She walked on autopilot as she recalled what had happened the night before.

She was no longer certain the evening counted as a *date*. She thought she'd been pretty clear regarding her intentions in her invite, but other than the brief moment Caleb had cuddled her against his chest as they'd looked at the heavens, he'd been disappointingly hands off. She didn't count the way he'd clutched her waist when they'd first headed out on the sled. Fear might be an aphrodisiac, but it wasn't the way she wanted to attract Caleb.

The clear skies that had allowed them to witness two more shooting stars also meant dipping temperatures and, by the time they returned the snowmobile to its shed and begun the drive home, she'd been glad to blast the heater to take the chill from her fingers and toes. Once at their duplex, he'd thanked her politely and vanished inside without even an attempt at a goodnight kiss, deserting her on her own front step, confused and frustrated.

Maybe she had misinterpreted their initial thrum of connection. On his part, at least. She still felt a buzz of sexual attraction, but it would die off soon if he showed no further interest.

She hoped.

Two hours of vigorous canine explorations later, Fergus was ready to head home. Grey clouds had slowly swept in during their walk, and a brooding stillness filled the air, along with the scent of snow. The forecast called for ten to fifteen centimetres overnight. If that happened, she might have to call one of her buddies to ask for a ride into work. As much as she loved her car, it really wasn't a winter vehicle.

She almost missed seeing the envelope tucked into the mailbox next to her front door. When Fergus was with her, she usually went into the house via the back and, as no deliveries came on weekends, she had no reason to check it. The flash of white caught her eye, though, and she hurried up the steps, retrieved the envelope, and then went to open the side gate for Fergus. He dashed into the yard to do the reconnaissance he felt necessary after any absence, and she made her way inside.

Her name was written on the outside of the envelope in Caleb's tiny, precise writing. Squelching down an unwelcome surge of nervousness, she took the time to remove only her boots and mittens before sitting down on a kitchen chair and opening it.

THE PROMISE OF FROST

Dear Luca,

I tried to come up with something as clever as your questionnaire, but struck out. I hope you'll accept this much less original invitation.

Would you be available for dinner on Tuesday evening? You mentioned that you'd never tried sushi, which I find reprehensible given the variety and excellence of the restaurants serving that delicacy in Prince George.

Thank you for last night. This city boy will never forget his first shooting star.

Caleb

He'd included his phone number under his name.

Fergus scratched at the door and she let him in absently, her thoughts tangled. She really hadn't expected this, not after the way last night had ended. And she really didn't want to find herself in yet another relationship that ran hot then cold and back again. She'd taken that train with Trent already and found it difficult to disembark.

The memory of Caleb's arms holding her as they stared at the stars tugged at her. His chin had brushed her temple, the faint scruff of his whiskers ruffling her nerves deliciously. There'd been *something* there, she knew it.

She dug her cell out of her pocket and tapped out his number.

CALEB STOOD AT LUCA'S front door on Tuesday and drew in a deep breath.

It had taken him less than twenty-four hours to succumb to the urge to invite her out for dinner, and he still wasn't entirely certain it was a good idea. His invitation had implied it was a simple thank you for the adventure on Saturday night, but honesty compelled him to admit more complex reasons lurked below the surface.

He'd disappointed her when he'd refused to wish on the falling star. She'd remained friendly and polite, but her eyes no longer gleamed with an unspoken promise, and he couldn't shake the feeling that he'd failed her. He told himself—repeatedly—that it didn't matter what she thought of him.

Obviously, he hadn't listened to his own advice. Given his current situation, standing on her stoop.

His knock set off ferocious barking from inside. If he didn't know Fergus was a scrawny mutt with long grey whiskers, a scraggly tail and whippy body, he would have pictured a slavering, red-eyed demon.

"I'll be right there," Luca called through the closed door. "I'm just putting Fergus out."

Still trying to settle his nerves, Caleb tucked his hands in his pockets and turned to survey the street as he waited. Christmas decorations bedecked most of the homes—red and green lights, inflatable snowmen, even a reindeer with a blinking scarlet nose. It was an older neighbourhood, with many duplexes like his and Luca's—low roofed, one-storey buildings with no covered parking. The house he, Teri, and Owen had shared—and the one she and his son still lived in—had boasted a two-car garage, two-point-five bathrooms, and more space than they really needed. But after the divorce Caleb had only cared about finding a well-maintained home at the lowest end of his price range. Any spare cash went into his new business and an emergency savings account. In a year or two, once things had settled, he might consider buying something else, but for now this was enough.

The door behind him clicked and he turned, already smiling, ready to greet Luca. His breath whooshed out in a stream of condensation and his eyes widened.

In deference to the freezing temperatures, Luca wore a hip-length woolen jacket in a rich blue, its wide belt snugged around her waist. A flat cap in a complementary shade covered her dark-brown hair at a jaunty angle, and a brightly coloured scarf wound around her chin and shoulders. Below the hem of her coat, her legs were bare before being protected by knee-high boots in shiny patent leather, with spiky heels that brought her two inches closer to his own five-foot-ten.

"You look—great," he said, too stunned to come up with a better word.

Her smile was blindingly bright. "Thanks. I don't get a chance to dress up often anymore. Wait until you see what's under the coat."

His mind short circuited, fizzing sparks at the word *under*. Speechless, he held out his hand and she took it, allowing him to help her down the icy stairs. "I haven't worn heels for a while. If I wobble like a newborn foal, that's why."

Seizing her explanation as the perfect excuse, he tucked her hand into the bend of his elbow and escorted her slowly and carefully past her green Smartie of a car to his much more sedate, five-year-old sedan. Still without speaking, he opened the passenger door and handed her in, then took the long way around the back of the car so he could suck in few extra deep breaths of chilly air before sliding behind the steering wheel.

It was ridiculous to be so bowled over by a completely clothed woman. It had to be because he was used to seeing her in casual or work gear. The sophisticated person next to him bore little resemblance to the labourer in a reflective vest or outdoor adventurer he'd met before.

He reversed out of the driveway, craning his neck to check for oncoming traffic. Every time he tried to slot Luca into the *friend and neighbour* category, she refused to stay there. He'd regretted not taking the opportunity to kiss her on Saturday from the moment he'd shut his own door behind him. Deciding to ask her out had made him feel like a teenager—sweaty, anxious, and lightheaded. He knew he wasn't ready for anything long-term, and definitely didn't want to expose Owen to more turmoil—but he couldn't get her out of his thoughts.

The silence thickened. *Say something,* he commanded himself. *Something intelligent, preferably.* What came out of his mouth was—

"How was your day?"

Well, it could have been worse.

"Not bad. I was out on the 600 Road, which made a nice change from hauling chips."

He halted at the stop sign at the end of their street, then turned right into the main stream of traffic. "What exactly is it you do?"

"I drive for Apex Transport. Short-haul work—chips to the pulp mills, wood waste to the bio-energy plant at the university, that sort of thing. Today I was out at a cut block getting loaded by the grinders out there."

"Don't take this the wrong way," he said slowly, "but I just want to be clear. You drive those enormous chip trucks?"

She grinned. "I'm used to that reaction. More and more women are driving truck, especially for companies like Apex. It's a physical job, but nothing out of the ordinary for someone in decent shape. And short-haul work is Monday through Friday, regular hours. Pays good, too."

"I knew you did something manual. I mean, I've seen you in your safety gear. I just didn't picture you driving a rig bigger than my house."

"You work from home, right?" she asked, and the rest of the drive was taken up by casual, get-to-know you chatter. Maybe it was odd they hadn't gotten to this at Summit Lake, but for some reason tonight felt more like a first date than that evening had.

Not a date, he reminded himself, then thought, *Ah, who the hell am I fooling?* Just because he hadn't decided where things might go with Luca didn't mean this wasn't a date. He still hadn't told Owen he was seeing her—his son would be back with him after school tomorrow, as this was his last night with his mom—and wasn't sure if he would.

Yet.

CHAPTER SIX

The atmosphere couldn't be more different than Saturday night, Luca thought with a smile as Caleb guided her into the restaurant. They were given seats at the sushi bar and she unwound her scarf as she looked around the room. Not worse, just different.

Even though it was barely five-thirty on a Tuesday, the restaurant was packed. The Asian-inspired decor was overlaid with Western Christmas displays—tinsel and baubles and even a brightly lit tree in the far corner. She squinted. Yup—it was topped with a large star made out of chopsticks and spray-painted gold. Servers wore cheerful red vests over white shirts, and strings of multi-coloured lights draped around the doors and windows.

But overwhelming it all was the Christmas-themed karaoke drowning out the chatter of diners and rattle of silverware. At the moment, two women were killing Mariah Carey's *All I Want for Christmas*—and not in a good way.

Caleb's expression was an interesting mix of appalled, apologetic, and amused. "I'm sorry," he said, his gaze drawn irresistibly back to the definitely-not-dulcet duo. "I had no idea it was karaoke night."

"This is great," Luca grinned. "I love karaoke."

"You do?" His tense shoulders tensed even more.

She laughed. "Don't worry. Listening to it, not participating." She unbuttoned her coat and shrugged out of it. "I watched *American Idol* for the auditions—the worse, the better. You probably think that makes me a horrible person."

She glanced toward him and stilled, one eyebrow raised. He swallowed, his Adam's apple bobbing.

"I'm sorry, what did you say?" His voice was low and rough. "I got distracted."

She'd chosen her dress carefully. The neckline revealed a-hair-past-modest amount of skin, and she considered the way the fabric clung to her breasts and framed her average-yet-adequate cleavage tantalizing. From Caleb's reaction, she was right.

Maybe it was because her day job required her to wear sexless, bulky protective gear that, when she got the chance, she enjoyed showing off her feminine side. The closet in her second, unused bedroom was crammed with silky dresses, short skirts, and seductive blouses. And no one knew about the sexy lingerie she wore under her work clothes every day.

Given the heated look in Caleb's eyes right now, however, she might let him in on that secret. It would be worth revealing it to make the fire she saw flickering in his pupils flare higher.

The attendant behind the bar approached, breaking the building tension between them. Luca took the offered menu and stared at it blindly for a moment, still caught in the delicious connection.

"How adventurous are you feeling?" Caleb said.

For a disorienting instant she wondered whether he was suggesting a make out session right here, right now. If he was feeling only half the attraction she was, it seemed perfectly logical. His next words dispelled that. Fortunately or unfortunately, she wasn't sure.

"They have all sorts of cooked options, if you're not up for raw. We can start with one or two dishes and go from there based on what you like."

She blinked, and then closed her menu. "You know what? You order whatever you think best. I promise to try at least one piece of everything, no matter how squiggy-looking."

SOMEHOW CALEB HAD KNOWN Luca wouldn't shy away from new experiences. She tried everything he put in front of her, and discovered—somewhat to her own surprise, she admitted—that she enjoyed them all. It was a leisurely meal and, though they'd arrived early in deference to Luca's work schedule, by eight-thirty she was yawning.

"I'm so sorry," she said. "I'm not used to going out on weeknights."

"Time to get you home," he said, making a *cheque please* gesture at the attendant.

Just outside the restaurant, they met three men on their way in. Caleb had his hand on Luca's arm and he immediately felt her stiffen.

Two of the men passed by with only casual glances, but the tallest of the trio stopped. "Luca," he said, a smirk crossing his face.

Well, maybe it was a smile, but something in his stance and expression made Caleb's skin itch.

"Trent." She nodded briefly and made to go around him. He stepped to the side, blocking her path, and Caleb's free hand formed a fist.

"How have you been?" Trent said, ignoring Caleb completely.

He was fine with the other man's indifference. It gave Caleb the chance to size him up. A couple inches taller than himself. Reasonably fit, though the suit under his unbuttoned coat stretched a little too tightly across his belly. Blond hair, blue eyes. Irritating grin unfazed by Luca's coolly civil expression.

"Fine." She uttered the short syllable with teeth-snapping brusqueness.

Seeming oblivious to her icy tone, he said, "You're looking good." He scanned Luca with a twist of his mouth that made Caleb want to apologize for all men, everywhere. "We should get together, have a drink. Catch up."

"That's not going to happen." Her reply was fast and certain, but Caleb still felt a tiny flair of jealousy. His brain understood why Trent might want to spend time with Luca—what rational man wouldn't?—but his gut didn't like the idea.

"We could celebrate my new promotion. I was just named Regional Manager."

"Congratulations. But no." Icicles dripped off Luca's voice, and she took a step forward. Again, Trent shifted just enough to block her path.

"Are you still driving truck?" he asked. A thread of amusement ran through his words, as if Luca's job was a joke. The guy was starting to get on Caleb's nerves.

"Yes." Her chin lifted a notch.

Trent shook his head. "You never understood how embarrassing it was that my girlfriend was a truck driver, as if she were a high school dropout."

Luca had *dated* this jerk? On the surface, the sophisticated, classy Luca he'd met tonight certainly matched Trent's worldly façade. But he couldn't picture her wasting time on such a condescending, conceited jackass.

Luca's retort was proud and fierce. "It's lucky I'm not your girlfriend anymore, then, isn't it?" Her defiance made Caleb want to kiss her, but he settled for shifting his hand from her arm to her back in silent support.

"Goodnight, Trent." Apparently deciding that *through* was the only way to go, Luca moved forward again. This time Trent stepped back, but with a smug look that made it clear he thought he was *allowing* her to go.

Caleb followed, giving Trent a hard stare as he went by. Luca didn't need him to defend her, but it wouldn't hurt to make sure the other man understood Caleb was on to him. He thought he heard a muttered curse, but was willing to give the jerk the benefit of the doubt in order to get Luca away.

Once inside the car and heading home, he risked a glance at her. She didn't appear upset, more thoughtful.

"Old boyfriend, I gather?" he said, keeping his tone light.

She shook her head, as if dismissing unwelcome thoughts. "Yes."

"A serious one?" It was like poking his tongue in a sore in his mouth—painful but impossible to stop doing.

"Is eight years together serious?"

He choked. "I would say yes?"

47

"I met him when I was twenty-four. We've been separated for more than a year now. Lived together for five."

He did the math. That made her nine years younger than him, and seven years younger than Teri. She was a good age to be a stepmother to Owen.

Whoa. Where did that *come from?*

Yanking his thoughts back to the conversation, he said vaguely, "I see."

"I thought of introducing you, but to be bluntly honest, I didn't want to. He's not worth getting to know." She sighed. "In my defense, when I first met him, he wasn't as irritating as he was tonight."

"He seemed a little...dismissive...of your career choice."

"Yes. And my choice of clothing and how I talked and what I liked to eat. He's a climber, socially and professionally, and I didn't fit into his image. He kept trying to convince me to take a secretarial job at his financial firm, but I like driving truck. I'm good at it." Her tone grew thoughtful. "Thank goodness I never gave in. *That* would have been awkward after we broke up."

He felt there were deeper issues she wasn't mentioning, and wanted to ask more questions, but didn't think he had the right. If she was willing to share, she would.

She wasn't, as evidence by her silence the rest of the journey.

Despite his best intentions not to let the opportunity for a goodnight kiss slip by a second time, he waved her into her home after nothing more than a squeeze of her hand.

Timing was a bitch.

GODDAMN, TRENT, Luca thought viciously as she scrubbed cleanser on her face, removing the light makeup she'd worn. What were the chances they'd meet tonight? And what was he playing at?

When she'd left him, he'd made it perfectly clear he thought she was making a big mistake. "Don't bother crawling back when you come to your senses," had been his exact words.

Now *he* was the one suggesting they get together for old time's sake?

Screw that.

She rinsed and dried her face and marched to her bedroom, Fergus at her heels. She'd been having a perfectly lovely time with Caleb and anticipating at least over-the-clothes petting before the evening ended. Yes, it was past her bedtime, but exploring the sparks that flared brighter every time their eyes met would have been worth missing some sleep.

Goddamn, Trent, she repeated, punching her pillow into shape, and flopping down onto the mattress. Fergus jumped lightly up and curled nose-to-tail at her feet. Minutes later he was whimpering and twitching in his sleep, while Luca still lay wide awake, fuming.

She had no intention of reconciling with Trent, but she could see how Caleb might have been put off by having her ex-boyfriend shoved in his face. Not that he'd been anything but polite and solicitous after. That was part of the problem.

She'd wanted a possessive kiss and lust-inducing caresses.

Instead, she'd gotten a handshake and a wave.

BRENDA MARGRIET

Goddamn, Trent.

CHAPTER SEVEN

Friday afternoon, Owen raced into the house, threw his backpack into the closet, tossed off his jacket, and kicked off his boots.

"Waldo! Where are you, Waldo?" he shouted, disappearing down the hall.

Oh, to have the energy of an eight-year-old boy, Caleb thought wryly.

School was now out for winter vacation, and his son would be spending the first part with him, but not the days of Christmas. Last year, though Caleb and Teri had been separated for months and the divorce almost final, they had wanted to give Owen a traditional holiday with both his parents. Despite their good intentions, it had been awkward and uncomfortable for everyone, so this year they had decided Owen would spend it with Teri only.

Caleb couldn't help but wonder what Luca's plans were for the holidays. He hadn't talked to her since Tuesday night, other than a friendly hello when they'd both arrived home at the same time one afternoon, she from work and he and Owen after a parent-teacher conference at school.

He *wanted* to see her again. But sometimes what he wanted wasn't what was best. He didn't think his first foray into dating post-divorce should be with a woman whose ex appeared intent on getting back together with her. It didn't matter that

Luca had showed no interest in the idea—it was still a complication he could do without. Also, the twinge of jealousy he'd felt had been an unwelcome reminder of the end of his marriage. Teri's infidelity had kicked his ego hard and, while he'd managed to get past it for Owen's sake, it would be stupid to put himself voluntarily into another embarrassing love triangle.

Clutching the kitten to his chest, Owen popped out of his bedroom. "Waldo and I are going to watch *Questology*," he said, naming his most recent television obsession.

"Okay. I'll be downstairs in my office," he said. With the way Teri's schedule worked out, Owen would be with her from three o'clock on Christmas Eve to three o'clock on New Year's Eve. It would be a long stretch of time without his son's poltergeist presence, so Caleb intended to enjoy these next few days as much as possible. He'd put in a couple hours every night after Owen was in bed to stay on top of things.

But before the vacation could begin, he had to wrap up a task or two that couldn't wait.

Caleb got a good hour's worth of work in, but still had a few loose ends to tidy up when Owen trailed glumly into his office and clutched his elbow. "I'm bored," he whined.

"Already?" This did not bode well for the next week. "Why don't you get your snowsuit on and we'll go sledding as soon as I'm done. Just five more minutes." It would be full dark by the time they got to the hill at a nearby park, but it was illuminated by streetlights and would make the rides that much more thrilling. "Maybe we'll pick up hamburgers on the way home. Celebrate the last day of school with junk food."

"Yeah!" Owen brightened and thudded up the stairs. At least he was still easy to amuse. Caleb was dreading the days when tobogganing with Dad no longer held the same attraction.

When Caleb surfaced again, the five minutes he had promised Owen had stretched to forty-five. He made his way hurriedly upstairs, thankful though slightly confused by Owen's forbearance in not interrupting him when he hadn't appeared as promised.

Waldo was sleeping in his cat tree but deigned to crack one eye as Caleb went past. Owen's snowsuit and boots were missing from the back closet, and he opened the door to let his son know he'd only be a minute more, expecting to see him playing in the snow.

Nothing but an empty expanse greeted him, the hollows of Owen's footprints tracking through the yard deep with twilight shadows.

His heart immediately swelled against his lungs, making breathing difficult.

Calm down, he told himself. *Maybe he's in the front.* Refusing to run, he paced deliberately to the front door. Owen was perfectly safe in the front yard. He knew to stay away from the street. And strangers.

Luca's bright green car was parked neatly in its slot next to his grey sedan, but no red and blue snowsuit was in view. The glittering lights twinkling from the ginormous snow globe squatting in front of the window taunted him.

"Owen!" Caleb bellowed, trying not to let terror overwhelm him. He *knew* there was a simple explanation. The odds of something...unwelcome...happening to his son were low. Thousands of kids played outside without supervision, and hardly any of them disappeared.

He felt a little faint.

This time he *did* run through the house. Owen *had* to be in the back yard. Caleb just hadn't seen him before. Stomping into his boots and yanking on his parka, he dashed out the door. "Owen!" he shouted again. "Owen!"

"Over here, Dad!" a distant but oh-so-loved voice piped up.

He gripped the stair railing, the icy metal searing into his unprotected skin, dizzy in relief. "Where are you?" he shouted back to his still invisible son.

"At Malcom's house. Behind Luca's."

Who the hell was Malcolm? Caleb thought as he strode through the snowy yard to the corner behind the tree Owen had climbed less than two weeks ago. Now the blood was no longer thrumming in panicked beats through his veins, he could hear the sound of blades on ice coming from the yard directly behind Luca's and kitty-corner to Caleb's.

He'd known parenthood would cause anxiety and worry. He just hoped the stress didn't kill him before Owen grew up.

Using the backer rail at the bottom of the fence, he raised himself enough to have an unimpeded view of the rink that stretched from one side of the neighbour's yard to the other. Owen raced around with short, choppy strides, Fergus skittering at his heels with a laugh on his doggie face, while Luca glided easily in sweeping motions.

Luca.

His relief at finding Owen safe and sound mingled with the shock of seeing her so unexpectedly. With his son. Who still didn't know his father had been on two dates with the neighbour he seemed to be befriending, all on his own.

Fergus noticed him first and raced to the fence, barking in friendly greeting. Caleb ignored him.

"What are you doing here?" he said. He'd meant to direct his question to his son, but his gaze was locked on Luca, and he wasn't surprised when she answered. Her eyes narrowed as she came to an abrupt stop, snow spraying up from her skate blades.

"I invited Owen to come skating," she said reasonably.

The panic-inspired adrenalin shifted seamlessly to feed his fury. "Without asking my permission?" he snapped. "I thought he'd been—" He bit off the rest of the sentence. He felt ridiculous enough, now he knew Owen was safe. He didn't need to make a bigger spectacle of himself.

"I told you I was here, Dad." Owen wobbled to a stop beside Luca. She reached out to steady him and Caleb's anger took on a jealous hue. He'd intended to take Owen skating sometime in the next few days. Now she'd stolen his thunder.

He was being irrational. He didn't care.

"I told you to get ready for tobogganing," he said, focussing his gaze on his son.

Owen nodded vigorously. "I know. I did. But then Luca saw me waiting outside and asked if I wanted to go skating on her friend's rink. I yelled down the stairs when I got my skates and helmet. I thought you heard me."

IF LUCA HADN'T HEARD the thread of fear in Caleb's voice when he'd first called his son's name, she might not have been willing to cut him any slack for his current behaviour. It reminded her unfavourably of the first time they'd met. But she had, and the joy and relief on his face when he'd appeared over the fence and seen Owen had only enhanced her sympathies.

He was obviously one of those people whose love and affection was sometimes expressed with a raised voice and nervous anger.

"I wouldn't have taken him if I hadn't thought you knew where we were," she said quietly. "He met me in the front and he and Fergus and I walked around the block. He wasn't out of my sight for a second."

The last tension drained out of Caleb's face. "I'm sorry I shouted, buddy," he said to Owen. His gaze flicked to hers, and she took it to mean she was included in the apology. "I didn't hear you when you came in. I guess I was too busy working."

"That's okay, Dad. Hey, look what Luca taught me!" He headed off, taking the corner with deliberate crossover steps, Fergus once again in pursuit.

"Good job," Caleb called out abstractedly. He was still gripping the top of the fence as if he needed support.

"I really am sorry if we gave you a fright," Luca said.

"It's okay."

She shook her head. "I imagine it's every parent's nightmare."

One corner of his mouth quirked up in wry acknowledgment. "I never thought I had an overactive imagination until I became a dad."

"Do you have skates?" she said impulsively. Since he hadn't bothered to get in touch since their sushi date, he was obviously no longer interested. She didn't blame him—their run in with Trent had probably made him doubt her sanity. What woman in her right mind would have stayed with such a man for eight years, after all?

She'd get over the inconvenient longings she still had for Caleb. Some day. But in the meantime, that didn't mean she couldn't be friendly. "Why don't you join us?"

"Are we even allowed to be here?" he asked. "I've never met these neighbours."

"Malcolm would love to know we're using his rink. He builds it for his grandkids every year. He and his wife are in Hawaii for a couple weeks but I have an open invitation to use it while they're gone."

He watched his son for a minute, then met her eyes, a small smile melting any remaining iciness from his expression. "I'll be right over."

CHAPTER EIGHT

The following Tuesday, Luca arrived home after a day of frenetic Christmas shopping to find yet another hand-delivered envelope in her mailbox. Her stomach gave an odd little swoop, but she let the anticipation build, forcing herself to unload her car, fuss over Fergus, and set the kettle to boil before retrieving it.

Since the ice-skating incident on Friday night, she'd received one other missive—an invitation to join them on the delayed sledding expedition. It had been written in the unformed hand of an eight-year-old boy, though the slightly stodgy wording had obviously been directed by his father.

The warmth it had engendered in her chest was both thrilling and terrifying.

She'd had to regretfully decline the invite, however, as it had coincided with previous plans. She opened today's envelope with interest.

Dear Luca,

Dad says today is the Winter Solstice, which is the shortest day of the year. We would like to invite you to celebrate by joining us for movies and popcorn starting at 7 o'clock. Please text Dad to let us know if you can come.

Your friend,

Owen

The salutation made her hesitate. She'd never been friends with a child before—well, not since she'd been one herself. It gave her a squishy feeling to realize that was how Owen saw her. He seemed a happy, well-adjusted kid, notwithstanding his meltdown on Friday night when Caleb had told him it was time to go home and he had disagreed...forcefully. He was also bright, funny, and affectionate. If she wasn't careful, she might fall in love with the little man.

And there was the rub.

That potential wasn't only restricted to the son. His father held an inescapable allure of a completely different nature. If Caleb only viewed her as a friend, how would she deal with it? She'd never been friends with a man that ignited the intensity of sexual attraction she felt for the older Frost. If she wanted something *more* with Caleb, and he didn't want the same thing, how would that affect Owen?

She shook her head, vexed at her thoughts. She was getting *way* too far ahead of herself. Yes, she fantasized about kissing Caleb, speculated whether the promise of attraction she felt might blossom into something more. But that was a problem for another day.

Tonight, she was going to accept an invitation from a friend.

THE PROMISE OF FROST

OWEN WAS ALREADY ENSCONCED in his nest, waiting rather impatiently to start the movie. "When is Luca coming, Dad?" he asked for the seventeenth time in fifteen minutes.

"She'll be here when she gets here, you wingnut. Give her a break. She's not late yet."

When Owen had asked if they could invite Luca sledding, Caleb had balked at first. On a personal level, he was still hesitant about Trent—his role in Luca's life and Caleb's own reaction to him.

But most importantly—he was worried his son could grow too attached to the woman next door. What would happen when Luca was no longer a part of their lives?

His resolve weakened by his son's puppy-dog eyes and his own enjoyment of the time they'd spent on the skating rink, he'd succumbed. Even forcing Owen to write an invite the old-fashioned way hadn't dampened his son's enthusiasm.

When Luca had regretfully refused the sledding invitation, Caleb had been surprised at the depth of his own disappointment. So much so that, when Owen had suggested trying again with movie night, he had barely blinked. He knew he had a habit of overthinking the little things. Luca had given no indication she'd noticed—or even cared—that Caleb had taken a step back since their sushi date. What would it hurt to keep her as a friend?

A knock sounded at the door and his heart thumped fiercely. *Friend*, he reminded the unruly muscle in his chest. *She's just a friend.*

"She's here, she's here! Can you get that?" Owen called. "Waldo's asleep on my lap."

Grinning at the rather adult tone his son employed, Caleb opened the door. "Welcome to movie night," he said, stepping back in the small entryway to make room for Luca to enter. "Owen's so glad you could make it." There was no need to mention his own delight.

Despite the freezing temperatures and gently falling snow, she hadn't worn a coat to cross the tiny distance from her home to his. The heavy bulky-knit sweater she wore over black leggings looked soft and touchable, and snowflakes spangled her short, dark hair.

"Thanks for inviting me." Her eyes gleamed with intoxicating intelligence, pink lips curving over white teeth. One incisor crossed just slightly over the tooth next to it.

His body stiffened in instant arousal.

So much for keeping her in the friend zone.

Shifting slightly to hide the evidence of his attraction, he kept his smile easy and focussed on hiding the rush of lust that flamed across his skin. Luckily, Luca's attention had been drawn away.

"Wow," she said, her eyes widening. "This is *fantastic.*"

With relief, he turned to survey the room. "What's movie night without a blanket tent?" he said, pleased at her reaction. He and Owen had spent most of the afternoon transforming the living room. Mismatched sheets and light blankets emblazoned with cartoon characters and team logos were stretched from wall to wall and held up by clamps and makeshift tent poles. Even the cat tree had been put into use. In the far corner, the Christmas tree was marooned in splendid isolation. Other than that, everything else was indistinguishable lumps and bumps.

"Come on in!" Owen's disembodied voice invited.

Dropping to her knees, Luca wasted no time crawling through the draped opening. Caleb remained standing, momentarily distracted by her wriggling ass.

"This is *awesome*," he heard Luca say in a wondering tone.

Swallowing, he said, "Do we want popcorn now or a little later?"

"Now!" two voices chorused, and the sense of rightness enveloping him grew stronger.

"As you wish," he said, and headed to the kitchen.

THE CREDITS STARTED to roll and Caleb used the remote to turn off the TV. Once it blinked out, the tent was lit by nothing more than the strings of fairy lights he had rigged to hang from the blankets that belled over their heads.

Luca rolled to her side, careful not to disturb Owen, blissfully asleep between her and Caleb, his little body radiating heat like a furnace. He'd only made it halfway through the second feature of the evening. She'd contemplated making her excuses and heading home then, but she'd never seen the animated Christmas movie he had chosen and she wanted to find out how it ended.

That was the only reason she stayed. It had nothing to do with not wanting the evening to end in general. Not at all.

"He's out like a light," she whispered.

Caleb rolled his head to look at her over his sleeping son. Cushions from the couch made a temporary mattress, and heaps of pillows formed a cozy backrest. If Luca concentrated, she could smell a hint of Caleb's cologne on the cotton pillowcase under her head, despite the lingering scents of hot buttered popcorn.

"I'm surprised he made it as long as he did. He's usually in bed by eight-thirty at the latest."

She didn't think he meant his comment as a hint, but it was as good a segue as any. "I guess I should go."

"You're not working tomorrow, are you?"

"No. I'm off until the new year."

His eyes were warm and direct, and a tingle of connection made her toes curl under the fleecy blanket Owen had insisted she use. She let her gaze drop to Caleb's mouth, linger for a moment, then lift. The spark she'd felt before kindled into something fiercer, brighter.

"Stay for a nightcap?" he said, his voice low and a little rough. She licked her lips and this time it was his gaze that fell. When he dragged it back up to meet hers, he added, "I'll put Owen in his bed first."

"All right." She wasn't exactly sure what she was agreeing to, but she knew she couldn't go home now. Not while this delightful edginess tickled her senses.

Owen made small snuffling noises as Caleb rolled him into his arms and wriggled out of the tent backwards. Waldo, who had been curled on the cushionless couch behind their head for most of the evening, stretched, jumped down, and followed them out. The boy must have woken for a moment because there was a muffled conversation, one voice deep and comforting, the other high pitched and querulous. Only one set of footsteps returned, though, and she heard the clink of glasses and glug of liquid.

Savouring the slowly building tension, she shifted under the enveloping canopy so she was sitting almost upright. Two hands appeared in the opening and the scent of excellent Scotch wafted in. Silently, she took the glasses, letting her fingers drift over Caleb's. She heard a hiss of breath and smiled.

He crawled back under, his head and shoulders brushing the precarious covering and setting it swaying. She waited until he was settled next to her, then handed him a glass.

"Cheers," she said, lifting her tumbler. "To my first ever blanket fort movie night."

"Cheers." He clinked his glass against hers and they took their first sips.

"Mmmm, this is good stuff." She breathed in the heady aroma, the kick of alcohol warming her belly almost as much as Caleb's quiet presence.

"I save it for special occasions," he said, his arm brushing hers as he lifted his glass to his mouth.

She leaned closer, nudging him with her elbow. "This is a special occasion?"

He turned his head and they were nose to nose. In the subdued lighting of the tiny, colourful bulbs lining the tent, shadows filled the hollows under his eyes and around his mouth. "You tell me."

She pressed her lips to his in answer.

CHAPTER NINE

She tasted of salt and oak and—unexpectedly—cinnamon. Her mouth urged his open, and he almost spilled his drink at the surge of lust and passion that engulfed him when her tongue touched his. Breaking the kiss, he wasted an ounce of very expensive Scotch by shooting it back in one gulp. Luca gazed in astonishment, and then did the same, tossing her glass to the side before launching herself onto his lap and gluing their mouths back together.

The dad part of his brain had a quick moment of *shit, I bet that spilled on the cushions*, before the man part of his brain went *never mind, if you're lucky, there will be even more of a mess to clean up later.*

Luca straddled his hips, her leggings a nearly nonexistent barrier to the heat of her body. He clutched her waist and her sweater was as soft as he'd imagined.

Who cares about the sweater? Touch her! his man brain commanded.

He groaned into her mouth as his fingers slipped under and brushed against the bare, silky skin of her ribs. She pushed against him, her lips devouring his, her breasts squashed with pliable heat against his chest.

Comfortable clothes were a requirement of a blanket tent movie night, and his cock had free rein to rise under his loose athletic pants. It bumped against her ass and Luca growled, shifting up and back enough so she could lower her core onto his groin and rub against him enthusiastically.

In the right circumstances, he would have been all for her zero-to-sixty response. He wasn't sure what he'd been expecting when he'd asked her to stay for a nightcap, but it hadn't been this all-encompassing urge to strip her naked and slam into her until they both found release.

Not with Owen a few steps away and no locked door between his son and the woman he *had* to stop caressing.

In a minute. As soon as he found the willpower.

Reluctantly, he slipped his hands from under her sweater and cupped her face, his thumbs brushing her cheekbones.

"No," she demanded in a fierce whisper, "put them right back where they were. A little higher, actually."

He laughed breathlessly. "Can't." Unable to cut himself off entirely, he nipped her lips in between each stuttering statement. "Owen. No door. Not a good time."

Her urgent movements slowed, though her hips kept circling in small jerks. His cock was still pressed between them, still sending greedy, desperate signals. She whimpered and dropped her head onto his shoulder.

"Right. Your son. Not appropriate." Her choppy sentences reflected his own brain-fogged speech. "God."

He couldn't stop touching her. His hands drifted up her spine to play with the tiny hairs on the back of her neck and she squirmed closer. Her palms were flat on his chest. He wondered if she could feel his galloping heart.

He cleared his throat. "That was..."

She sat up slowly, settling her weight heavier on his groin. His hips lifted instinctively and her thighs gripped his, her eyes closing briefly. "Unexpected?" she said.

"No." Her eyebrows rose at his adamant tone. "Not unexpected. I've wanted to kiss you for a while now. I might not have imagined it would be quite so"—he paused again, searching for the right word; she had really scrambled his brain—"explosive."

"This is new territory for me, too." Her fingertips smoothed the soft cotton of his T-shirt and he couldn't restrain a shiver. "I don't usually get this hot and heavy after one kiss. I kind of jumped your bones."

She wasn't meeting his eyes and he realized she was embarrassed. He tipped her chin up with his loosely curled fist. "I didn't put up much of a fight."

Her mouth curled in a wry smile. "I didn't give you much of a chance."

"Luca. I'm a grown man. If I didn't want you right where you are right now, I'd do something about it."

She stiffened and bolted off his lap, as if suddenly aware of their intimate position. "Sorry. You wanted to stop, and I didn't even get off you."

He sat upright, ducking his head to avoid the blanket ceiling. They were conducting their conversation in whispers, in deference to Owen just down the hall, but that didn't stop him from speaking forcefully. "I didn't *want* to stop. Are you kidding me?" He made a futile gesture at his erection, tenting his loose pants eagerly. "Does this look like I don't want you?"

She giggled, amusement chasing the hint of humiliation away. "I guess not."

"Exactly. And it's damn uncomfortable, let me tell you. This is the first female contact I've had in more than a year."

"Really?" If anything, the laughter in her eyes grew. "More than a year?"

"Almost two. And it's not funny," he said, though he couldn't help an answering smile from spreading across his face. "The myth of the sexy single dad is just that. Most women I've met since my divorce aren't all that excited about taking on an eight-year-old boy, too." Not that he'd tried too hard to find one. Or at all.

For some reason, he didn't want Luca to know that. It would make whatever they had just shared more important, somehow.

"Well, they don't know what they're missing." She ran her fingers over the shell of his ear and down his neck. "I know you and Owen are a package deal. And I have no problem with that. None at all."

He might have been able to deal with the passion they obviously shared and still keep their relationship casual. But the affection in her voice when she spoke of Owen felled him like an axe to a sapling.

He was in so much trouble.

BETWEEN MOUTHFULS OF popcorn and telling Luca what was going to happen next in the movie, Owen had artlessly invited her to his and Caleb's early Christmas celebration. "This year I get Christmas Day with Mom, so Dad and I are pretending Christmas Eve is Christmas. We're going to get up early and open presents just like for real." Solemnly, he'd added, "Santa won't come here, 'cause he knows I'm going to be at Mom's, and I only get one present from him. But that's okay. I understand."

His casual acceptance had cracked her heart, and she'd had to resist the urge to hug him close. It spoke volumes to the commitment Caleb and his ex-wife shared in making Owen's life happy and stable, however.

Getting to know Owen was making her wonder about having a child of her own. She'd thought about it on occasion, with no sense of urgency, though once she'd turned thirty those occasions had come closer together and with more force. *Rather like contractions,* she thought wryly. But Trent had wanted to wait, and she'd been happy enough with that plan. Then, when they'd broken up, she'd been relieved there were no children to worry about.

Understanding Christmas Eve would be a special time for father and son, she'd gently declined Owen's offer. Even though she felt a longing to see Christmas through the eyes of a child once more, she knew she would be a fifth wheel in their private celebration.

Of course, that had been before the-kiss-that-rocked-her-world.

Christmas Eve morning, Luca stood at her kitchen window sipping her coffee and watching Fergus inspect the back yard. He'd worn a path in the snow along the fence line and patrolled it diligently multiple times a day.

Her stomach and toes still tingled when she relived those few stolen moments with Caleb under the blanket tent. She'd known she was attracted to him, but had had *no* idea the simple pressure of her mouth on his would send her rocketing into the stratosphere. She'd lost all sense of composure and only came to an awareness of her surroundings when he'd reminded her of Owen's innocent, nearby presence.

One kiss from Caleb had blown all her expectations out of the water. If they ever got naked together—

Well, they'd better be somewhere private, because she had a feeling she would be making *a lot* of noise.

Though she had seen neither the big nor little Frost since then, she felt no sense of abandonment or neglect. Just like the presents she unwrapped with excruciating deliberation, whatever she and Caleb might have together was worth waiting for. She didn't need the constant reassurance of daily contact.

As she let Fergus back in, along with a rush of icy air, she checked the time. Owen had said they were getting up early to open their presents, and she didn't want to intrude too soon. But nine o'clock seemed a reasonable time to bring over the last-minute gifts she'd picked up the day before.

She slipped into her boots and jacket. The temperature had dropped to a bitter thirty degrees below and even the quick trip to Caleb's would freeze the hairs in her nostrils. Gripping the handles of two gift bags in one fist, she opened the front door.

To find Trent standing on the stoop, hand raised to knock.

CHAPTER TEN

O wen lay on his stomach on the living room floor, teasing Waldo by dragging the mouse on a string the kitten had been given through the wrapping paper still strewn about. The mess made by opening presents was half the fun of Christmas, Caleb had always thought, his neat-freak tendencies in abeyance these few short hours a year.

He sat sideways on the couch placed under the wide window overlooking the front yard, his spine propped up on the armrest, his feet—enormous and furry in the Chewbacca slippers that had been Owen's gift—stretched out before him. His third cup of coffee was beginning to counteract the early start to the day, but he was still too groggy to do more than wonder vaguely who owned the SUV that pulled into Luca's driveway—until Trent stepped out, carrying a plastic-wrapped bouquet of flowers.

Irritation worked better than caffeine to clear away the remaining cobwebs. Sitting up so he could get a better view around the giant snow globe blocking much of the window, Caleb watched Trent stride past Luca's green beetle of a vehicle and out of sight along the path leading to her house. Without considering how ridiculous he might look, he shifted to his knees and pressed his cheek to the window, just in time to see Trent disappear inside.

He dropped back onto the cushion, balancing his coffee mug carefully, and scowled at the pair of toothy faces staring back at him from his toes.

He hadn't exactly forgotten about Trent. But the sight of Luca, warm and rumpled and sexy as she'd grinned at him over Owen's sleeping form, had made it so easy to push aside the logical reasons—of which Trent was only one—any deeper relationship between them was a mistake. To ignore everything in the moment except her, the touch of her mouth, the feel of her skin.

He had no right to be jealous that Trent was visiting Luca, he scolded himself. She owed Caleb no loyalty, had made him no commitments. It was ridiculous to compare her to his wife.

He'd been blindsided by Teri's infidelity, could still feel the shock and disorientation when she'd told him she wanted a divorce. Looking back with the knowledge he now had, he realized he should have seen the signs. But he hadn't, and he felt guilty about that. He should have noticed she wasn't happy, was feeling restless. After all, he'd loved her once. He should have been paying more attention.

Not that he thought he could have saved the marriage, even if he had. That took two people, working for the same goal. And if he was being brutal, he could admit he hadn't exactly been trying too hard to keep their relationship strong, either. Having an affair had never crossed his mind, but unease and dissatisfaction had been growing in him, and he'd simply shoved it away.

Trent was still inside with Luca. Caleb scowled.

LUCA BREATHED IN DEEPLY through her nose and then let the air out in one long, slow swoosh.

"No, Trent," she said for what felt like the millionth time. "I have no interest in getting back together. It's been more than a year since we broke up. Why on earth would you think I might even consider the idea?"

"There's no one else like you, Luca," he said. The roguish twinkle in his eye that used to melt her panties now seemed forced and fake. "Believe me, I've looked. Besides, it's Christmas. You don't want to be alone for the holidays, do you?"

Now his renewed interest made sense. "Getting shot down, are you?" she said with no compunction for his ego. "No date to bring to all the work parties and too embarrassed to go stag?" This time of year had always been important to Trent due to the number of social functions he attended, masking his ambition and greed behind the smiles and laughter of the holiday season. He'd admitted to Luca more than once he prospected more business during the two weeks of Christmas than many other months of the year.

His eyes narrowed. "It's not like that. I've dated lots of women since we broke up. But I don't like any of them as much as I liked you."

His use of the past tense didn't escape her. She pressed a hand melodramatically to her chest. "Be still my beating heart. What a romantic devil you are. The answer is still no." God, it felt good to stand up to him. It might have taken her longer than it should to get to this stage, but she revelled in it now.

"Luca—"

She thrust the bouquet of frostbitten, grocery store flowers back into his hands—his pathetic attempt at a gift had done nothing to support his cause—and reached past him to open the door. She hadn't wanted to let him inside at all, but the arctic chill had made that necessary when he wouldn't budge the first three times she'd asked. "Goodbye, Trent. For good. I mean it."

He put up a bit more of a fuss, but she finally shooed him out, closing the door with a resounding thud and leaning against it. Fergus regarded her with a quizzical expression, his chin resting on the arm of the couch. "I don't get it, either," she said. "If he'd been as determined to save the relationship as he seems to be to renew it, we might still be together."

A cold chill ran down her spine. If she hadn't left Trent, she would never have met Caleb and Owen.

Just the possibility carved a black hole in her heart.

A quick peek out the window revealed Trent was well and truly gone. Once more gripping the handles of the two gift bags, she relaunched her aborted mission.

Her knock on Caleb's front door was answered by childish shouts. Owen flung it open, dressed in rumpled Batman pajamas, his hair uncombed, and a smear of jam on his cheek.

"Merry early Christmas!" Luca resisted the urge to lick her thumb and clean the boy's face. *Huh, who knew? It must come with two X chromosomes*, she thought with amusement.

Owen zeroed in on the bags in her hand. "Are those for me?"

Caleb appeared, coming round the short wall that separated the living room from the entrance hall. "Owen!" he said, his tone sharp with disapproval. "That's not polite."

"It's okay," Luca said. She held out one of the bags. "This one is for you."

Owen took the gift eagerly. "Cool!"

Caleb smiled, but it didn't reach his eyes. His stern demeanour was somewhat undermined by the furry brown slippers encasing his feet. "What do you say, Owen?"

"Thank you! Can I open it now?"

"Of course." Luca grinned as the boy disappeared into the living room. She turned her attention back to Caleb. Wrinkles of irritation still creased his brow. She felt a moment of unease. "You're not upset I brought him a gift, are you?" she said. "It's nothing much."

"No, of course not." The denial appeared more automatic than sincere.

"I brought one for you, too." She held out the other bag with both hands, supporting the heavy bottle of Scotch inside. "Merry Christmas."

For a moment, their gazes locked. He seemed to be seeking something in her face, but she had no idea what. On a sigh, the furrows in his forehead smoothed out and his shoulders relaxed. "Thank you," he said. His fingers brushed hers as he took the gift. "Come on in. We have something for you, too."

She stripped off her outerwear and followed him into the living room, scuffling through the discarded wrapping paper strewn about. "It looks like Christmas was a success."

He tossed a more natural looking smile over his shoulder and took a small box from under the tree. "Some day you'll have to come over when the house doesn't look like it's been vomited on. Here." He thrust the box at her. "Coffee?"

"Sure. Thanks." She took a seat on the couch.

He waded through the debris and returned quickly with a mug. Owen was already engrossed in the small Lego kit she'd chosen. He was the first eight-year-old she'd ever bought a present for, but had figured she couldn't go wrong with a classic.

Caleb placed her coffee on the low table in front of the couch, then sat next to her, leaving a good foot between them. As much as she wanted to touch him, feel his heat against her skin, she knew now was not the time. Owen would be spending the next week with his mother. There would be plenty of opportunities then to explore whatever it was she and Caleb shared.

"You first," Caleb said, jerking his chin at the box on her lap.

"I wasn't expecting anything," she said. "Thank you." She hadn't been sure their relationship was at the level that allowed an exchange of gifts, but had decided she wanted to give one to Owen, which meant she couldn't ignore Caleb. Thank goodness she had, or this moment would have been rather awkward.

With a fingernail, she picked at the tape securing the rather clumsily folded paper. Cautiously peeling it back, she set to work on the next piece of tape.

"Oh, my god. You're one of *those* people," Caleb said.

She lifted her glance. This time, the smile in his voice was warmly reflected in his brown eyes. Her breath caught, and then she went back to her painstaking work. "You say it like that's a bad thing."

"If I'd had to guess, I would have thought you be an all-in, tear it off right away kind of woman."

He *had* to be referring to the way she'd attacked him under the blanket tent, but she ignored the innuendo and concentrated on releasing the wrapping. Finally, she revealed the rectangular, flat white box inside.

By this time, Owen had noticed what was going on, and was kneeling at her feet, squirming with impatience. "Open it!" he commanded.

She ruffled his hair and then did as she was told. "Oh," she said with sincere pleasure.

CHAPTER ELEVEN

"It's you and Fergus," Owen explained unnecessarily. "Do you like it?"

"I love it." A rustic wooden frame with pokerwork evergreens and mountains along the wide bottom edge held a candid photo of Luca and Fergus sitting in profile, Luca laughing, Fergus' ears perked and alert, both of them watching something happening out of frame. It took her a moment to realize it had been shot the afternoon they'd skated on Malcom's rink. "I don't remember you taking this," she said, directing her question to Caleb but not looking away from the gift.

"I was snapping a few of Owen, and happened to notice you both sitting like this." She felt his shrug. "I hope you don't mind."

"No, it's great." Impulsively, she leaned over and hugged Owen, still crouched at her knee. His thin, wiry arms wrapped around her neck without hesitation and she felt a swell of tenderness. When she released him, he scrambled back to his Lego, which Waldo had been regarding with active suspicion, and she turned to Caleb.

"Thank you," she said. "Fergus is like family. I love it." Her fingers itched to touch Caleb's unshaven cheek, to lean in and kiss him.

His gaze drifted from her eyes to her mouth and back up again, as if he shared her longing. "You're welcome." His lips quirked in a wry smile. "I'm going to be making waffles soon. Want to stay for brunch?"

DECEMBER 25TH WAS JUST another day on the calendar. So why did it feel so bleak when he couldn't spend it with Owen?

Caleb knew it was best for everyone he was no longer stuck in an unhealthy marriage. But having less time with his son was a heavy price to pay for that freedom.

The day might have been easier to bear if he had someone to share it with. Sure, he was currently surrounded by his loud and boisterous family, but it wasn't the same. He wanted—needed—someone who was here for *him*.

Someone like Luca. Someone who made him laugh and challenged his set ways and stirred his nerves into fizzing delight. But she was spending the day with her family. He didn't blame her, of course. Yet he couldn't help *wishing*...for what, he didn't want to articulate, even in the privacy of his mind.

At least he'd stopped fooling himself. Luca wasn't a friend. She was definitely something more. And while Owen would always be a priority, that didn't mean he couldn't figure out a way to fit Luca in, too. He knew she'd understand that Owen had to come first.

As he sat in his parent's living room, watching his nieces and nephews squabble with friendly heat over a card game, he wondered what Luca was doing at this moment. During brunch yesterday they'd swapped family trees. Her parents were going on forty years together, and she had a brother and sister, both younger than her, and no nephews or nieces. That compared to his parents who had just celebrated their fiftieth anniversary and his two sisters—he was the middle child—both of whom had a husband, a son, and a daughter.

"Oof, I'm stuffed." His younger sister Janice dropped onto the couch beside him with an inelegant sigh. "I shouldn't have had that second piece of pie."

"Well, you are eating for two. Again." He reached out and patted her rounded belly.

"I'm as big with this one at three months as I was with Caitlyn at seven," Janice moaned.

"You look great." Pregnancy agreed with his sister, unlike Teri who'd been sick the entire nine months. He'd wanted at least one sibling for Owen, but she'd said she needed time to forget how awful the whole process had been before even considering another child. As things had turned out, that had probably been for the best.

"It's too bad Owen isn't here," Janice said.

He huffed a wordless agreement. "I brought him by yesterday before dropping him off at Teri's so Mom and Dad could have some time with him, see him open their present."

"That's good. I know they appreciate that."

Caleb shifted, his conscience prickling. "Is it stupid to feel like I've let them down?"

Janice looked at him, eyes wide in surprise. "Mom and Dad?"

He gestured at their parents, sitting side by side on the matching love seat, laughing as they watched four of their five grandchildren play. "Fifty years, Jan. They made it *fifty years*, and I didn't get to ten."

"Do you really think they'd rather you stay in a broken marriage than be happy?" Janice said, scorn for her idiotic brother evident. "You'll find someone, Caleb. The *right* someone."

"I'm almost forty-two," he said, as if she didn't know. "I'm running out of time."

"To have fifty years with someone, maybe. But not to be happy." She patted his thigh. "Don't give up. You got burned once, but that doesn't mean you're destined to be a bachelor the rest of your life."

Luca came to mind once more. She was never far from his thoughts these days. He hadn't told her he'd seen Trent, though there had been plenty of chances to do so during brunch yesterday. Not that he had the right to say anything, anyway. She'd clearly sent her ex off with a flea in his ear, given the man's stiff and angry posture, the bouquet of flowers still dangling from his hand, and the way he'd slammed his car door before reversing out of the driveway with little heed for oncoming traffic. But the jealousy Caleb had felt had taken longer to recede than it should have, and his reaction had scared him.

Teri had hurt his pride, but he had the uneasy feeling Luca could break his heart.

LUCA REALIZED SOMETHING was missing from the Tannon family Christmas celebrations—children.

Christmas was for kids, a fact she'd known with her head but only realized with her heart after spending time with Owen. All through brunch yesterday, he'd been bubbling over with excitement about what Santa might bring, the gifts he'd get from his grandparents and aunts and uncles. He was the perfect age for the holiday—young enough to believe, not yet old enough to doubt.

As much as she loved her family, she now had an inkling why her parents suffered from grandparent fever.

"Danielle and I have something to tell everyone," Niki said, breaking into Luca's musings. Her sister gripped her girlfriend's hand and smiled besottedly. "We're engaged."

Shrieks and cheers erupted. Luca's mother jumped out of her chair to embrace both women, while her more sedate father simply said, "I'll get more wine. We need to toast." Her brother slapped Danielle on the back and tweaked his sister's ear. Tears filled Luca's eyes at the uncomplicated joy in the couple's faces.

That was love. *That* was what she wanted in her next relationship. There had to be *joy*.

She offered her congratulations and joined in the toast to future happiness with sincerity and pleasure.

And not a small lick of envy.

She'd done her best to distract herself from Caleb's absence all day, yet he'd surfaced again and again in her thoughts. Thinking about children and Christmas—which automatically led to Owen—hadn't helped, and neither had her sister's announcement.

Suddenly, she had the overwhelming urge to speak with him. Without pausing to consider consequences, she excused herself from the table, leaving everyone eagerly discussing wedding plans. Climbing the stairs to the second floor, she locked herself in the bathroom for even more privacy and dialled his number.

"Hello, Luca," he said, answering after only one ring. The low, welcome timbre of his voice soothed the worst of her agitation.

"I hope you don't mind. Me calling you, I mean. When you're with your family." Staring at herself in the mirror, she pulled a face at her incoherence. *Smooth, Luca.*

"No, it's good. Just a second, let me go into the sunroom." A brief silence, then, "I'm glad you called."

"You are?" she blurted. "Why?"

"Would it be weird if I said I missed you?" His puzzled tone matched her own slightly bewildered feelings. "Why did you? Call, that is."

"I guess I missed you, too," she echoed. Biting her lip, she added, hoping it wasn't too much honesty, too soon, "I wanted to hear your voice."

A humming silence filled the speaker. Before she could make a joke, retract her pathetic statement, Caleb said, "Everything okay?"

The caring in his voice burned the back of her throat and she swallowed. "Of course. It's great. My sister just got engaged."

"Congratulations?" The upward lilt encouraged further confidences.

"Niki's girlfriend is great. We all love Danielle." She fiddled with the towel hanging on the rack. "I guess I was just feeling a little...left out."

"I saw Trent at your place yesterday," Caleb said, a new clipped tone in his voice.

She frowned. "You did?" What did that have to do with anything?

"I wasn't spying. I just happened to look out the window. I thought you should know. And you don't have to tell me—"

Light dawned. She cut Caleb off. "You won't see him at my place ever again. I think I made it perfectly clear—one more time—we are through. The holidays make everybody crazy." Even herself. Enough soul searching. "What are you up to tomorrow?" she said, her voice infused with cheer as she thought about Caleb's interest in Trent. Was it possible he was a teensy bit jealous? She grinned.

"I was going to do some work," Caleb said. "I need to catch up after taking the time off with Owen this week."

"Is it vital? Can you put it off a little longer?"

"I suppose. What are you thinking?"

"Ever done a polar bear dip?"

CHAPTER TWELVE

"You are insane. Certifiably mentally unstable. And everyone else here along with you."

"*You're* here," Luca said, grinning. How had he never noticed how maniacal her smile was?

Caleb still wasn't sure how she'd managed to convince him to register for this deranged, preposterous event. Sure, it was for a good cause—a local charity that supported children with cancer—but he could have just written a cheque.

Yet here he was, standing on the edge of a frozen lake, watching crazy people jump into the frigid, black water revealed by a ten-metre square hole cut into the metre deep ice.

Luca had explained the Boxing Day Polar Bear Dip was an annual city tradition. Sometime during the twenty years he'd lived in Prince George he must have heard of it, as it had been going on much longer than that. He'd probably blocked the knowledge from his mind, like any rational human being.

"We're lucky it warmed up," Luca said. "They cancel it if the temperature is as cold as it was a couple days ago."

Caleb stared at her in disbelief. "Lucky?" He sounded like Owen, his tone thin and squeaky. Thank god his son wasn't here. Caleb had the sneaking suspicion he'd be first in the water.

"Where's your sense of adventure?" Luca said. "I've always wanted to do this, but couldn't find anyone brave enough to come with me."

For *anyone*, Caleb read *Trent*. Now he *had* to jump. He couldn't give Luca a reason to compare him to her irritating ex.

"Fine," he said between gritted teeth. Gritted in part to stop them from chattering. "Let's get this over with."

"Meet you back here in five minutes," Luca said, eyes sparkling. "We're really going to do this!"

Two large tents near the shore served as warming huts and changerooms. Caleb undressed and pulled on his swim trunks, stepped into a sacrificial pair of running shoes, and donned his housecoat. After savouring the sensation of life-giving warmth from the propane heater for a few more seconds, he tightened his belt, grabbed the stack of towels Luca had instructed him to bring, and headed back outside.

God*damn*, it was cold.

Luca was already waiting for him, bouncing on her toes, feet clad in aquatic socks, body wrapped in a huge, oversized robe. She must have read the trepidation in his expression, as her wide smile faded. "You're not backing out on me, are you?"

"I'm not sure what I did in a past life to deserve this," he said, spreading one towel onto the ice as Luca had and stepping onto it, "but no, I'm not backing out."

The blazing excitement that lit her entire being was worth the biting cold nipping at his knees and chasing its way up the baggy legs of his swim trunks to more sensitive bits.

"Don't think about it," she instructed. "On the count of three, drop your robe, run, and jump."

He was already frozen. The inky blackness of the water, churned up by the shrieking people taking their dips before them, yawned like a deadly abyss. "What if my heart stops?"

he said, not entirely joking. He'd heard the shock of cold water could do that.

"That's what the First Aid volunteers are for." Luca waved blithely at four men and women, one on each corner of the square, wearing the uniform of the St. John Ambulance.

"I noticed you didn't say it *won't* happen," he muttered. But in the face of Luca's unflagging enthusiasm, he knew he'd run out of excuses. God*damn* it!

"On three," he said.

She grinned at him, her whole face lit with glee, devilry, and anticipation. "One."

"Two," he said.

"Three!" She dropped her robe.

In any other circumstance, seeing Luca in a bathing suit would have been arousing. Right now, his testicles were trying to crawl back into his body.

He shrugged out of his housecoat a second after her, and before he knew it, she'd grabbed his hand and was running toward the icy pool. He had time for one more fervent curse before she led him off the edge of the ice and he was enveloped in water so cold that he forgot how to breathe.

He felt flayed, abraded, as if someone was viciously rubbing his skin with diamond grit sandpaper. His limbs refused to respond to his brain's shrieking commands to swim, get out, escape.

Struggling to overcome the shock, he was one instant away from a panic attack when his head broke the surface. He gasped in life-giving air. Treading water, he wiped his face and opened his eyes, searching for Luca. A second later she popped out of the depths, her short cap of hair sleeked to her skull, her eyes huge and wide.

"Holy *shit*," she said. "That's cold!" She frantically splashed her way to the edge and he followed. Helpful hands dragged them out and they dashed to their waiting towels.

He'd done some research last night on polar bear plunges. It turned out there were proven benefits for healthy people to take part in such a stunt, which had reconciled him to joining Luca. He hadn't quite believed, however, that an icy water dip could give you an endorphin high.

Until now. He actually felt *warm* and giddy and like he could take on the world. From the glow on Luca's face and her babbling commentary as she scrubbed herself dry, she felt the same. One long stride in his soaked sneakers brought him close enough to wrap his arms around her and drag her body against his.

LUCA HAD NEVER FALLEN for the Canadian schoolyard dare of sticking her tongue to a metal surface on a bitterly cold winter day. But she thought if she had, it might be likened to the searing sensation of Caleb's lips melding with hers as they stood on a frozen, snow-covered lake.

He should have been cold. Instead, his kiss blazed her lips incandescently, his naked chest scorching through the soaked material of her swimsuit. Her breasts swelled and swirling heat fired low in her belly.

"Take that inside," a cheerful voice called out, jolting them apart. One of the St. John Ambulance volunteers stood nearby, grinning. "I know it doesn't feel like it, but hypothermia is still a possibility. Go warm up and then"—he winked—"go warm up, if you know what I mean."

Luca burst into laughter, still riding the adrenaline rush of surviving the plunge. Caleb pressed his mouth firmly to hers once again, a promise of more to come, and then they hurried into their respective tents.

Putting on warm, dry clothing had never felt more luxurious. Luca just about purred as she pulled on fleece-lined leggings, thick socks, and a thermal turtleneck, and then topped it all with layers and layers of outerwear. A volunteer handed her a to-go cup filled with hot chocolate and she headed outside.

Caleb was waiting for her, equally bundled up, his bag slung over his shoulder and a matching cup in his hands.

"That. Was. Awesome." She pressed a kiss to his chilly cheek. "Thank you so much."

"You're welcome. But just so you know"—the stern, unforgiving lines of his face were belied by the smile in his eyes—"I am *never* doing that again. You are on your own from now on. I'll stand by with towels and a hot drink, but that's it."

The warmth of the hot chocolate sliding down her throat was nothing compared to the glow Caleb's words engendered. He was talking about being with her in the future—*far* into the future, since one polar bear dip a winter was enough even for her. Her stomach tingled at the possibilities stretching between them.

He pointed toward a circle of people gathered around a fire crackling at the shoreline. "Want to warm up there before we leave?"

She tilted her head, studying him.

"What?" he said.

"Those projects you said you needed to get to. Can they wait a couple more days? If you worked in an office, you'd have tomorrow and Tuesday off, since the stats fall on a weekend this year."

His eyes narrowed in suspicion. "I am not committing to anything until you tell me what you're planning. If I'm not careful, you'll have me scaling Mount Everest."

"Now you're giving me ideas." He actually blanched and she laughed. "Don't worry. It's nothing so drastic. My family has a cabin at a small lake southwest of town." A thought struck her. "I can't believe I didn't make the connection before. It's on Frost Lake. You're Caleb Frost. Huh."

He made a *go on* gesture. "And you mention this because..."

"Do you want to go out there with me? Owen's with his mom until the afternoon of New Year's Eve, right? And no one in my family is using it for the next few days."

His gaze intensified. He knew what she was suggesting. Time alone. Together. No interruptions. Still, he said warily, "To clarify, this cabin has walls and a roof and some form of heat, right?"

His mistrust was rather endearing. "Yes. But no running water, just an outhouse."

"I assume there's no cell service there? Even though Owen's with Teri, I don't like to be out of touch."

How could she *not* be attracted to a man so dedicated to his son's welfare? "We can make sure she has my dad's contact info. If it's an emergency, he can drive out and get us. It's not even an hour and a half away."

"I don't know." He sipped his hot chocolate, his expression undecided.

"I'm sure Teri is perfectly capable of taking care of her son without your assistance for a couple of days." She touched her fingertip to the hollow of his throat, which was the only skin other than his face exposed to the elements. "It's not even noon yet. It will only take a couple hours to get organized. We might even get there before dark." She trailed her finger up the column of his neck, along his jaw to the sensitive skin under his ear. She felt him swallow.

She licked her lips and his eyes followed the movement. Electricity flashed between them, warming away the last vestiges of their frigid dunking.

"Just us," she reminded him. "All alone. No one to disturb us."

Caleb hiked his bag higher onto his shoulder, grabbed the wrist of the hand now tickling his earlobe, and tugged her toward the parking lot.

"Let's go," he said.

CHAPTER THIRTEEN

"There is no way your car could ever survive this," Caleb said, clutching the door handle and bracing his feet against the floor of the pickup. Actually, he wondered if *he* would survive unscathed. The truck bounced and shuddered its way up the steep, narrow, snow-covered track, jolting every vertebra in his spine.

Fergus, curled up on the back seat of the pickup, whined in seeming sympathy.

"It does okay in the summer if I'm careful. But I would never try at this time of year. Dad doesn't mind if I borrow his truck." Luca handled the heavy vehicle with a terrifying casualness. Of course, it was a lot smaller than the rigs she drove for work. "Four-wheel drive is the only way to go in winter."

Dusk was already falling, the trees lining the narrow path looming charcoal-grey against the inky sky. They had left the main highway heading south of Prince George around two-thirty and then driven west along a secondary road. Several kilometres in, what had begun as a properly paved route had degenerated into gravel. It was still wide and had been recently cleared of snow, but had been rutted with sections of teeth-jarring washboard.

Compared to the lane Luca was now manoeuvring, it might have been a German autobahn.

"Not much farther," she said.

Caleb's molars clacked together as the pickup dropped into a deep pothole, despite the fact they were creeping at a speed slower than he could walk. Remembering Luca's previous ideas of *not much farther*, he prepared for ages more of the rattling ride.

This time, however, she was telling the truth. Thirty seconds later she navigated one more corner, and the truck's headlights swept over a rustic cabin before losing themselves in the infinity of a wide, white expanse.

Frost Lake. He felt a totally unexpected sense of proprietorship as he caught his first glimpse of his namesake.

Luca parked the pickup at the foot of the steps leading to the door. The cessation of movement was a welcome relief and Caleb relaxed his death grip on the door handle. When she killed the engine, the silence that settled over them had the feeling of after midnight, not late afternoon. At Summit Lake, highway sounds had been faintly audible and lights from cabins had rimmed the shore. Here, there was nothing beyond the ticking of the cooling motor and the slowly deepening gloom.

And Fergus' frantic yipping and growling. He scratched at the rear door and wriggled his back end so vigorously Caleb felt the breeze from his tail.

"We're lucky there hasn't been too much snow this year," Luca said, reaching for the latch on her door. "It'll only take a minute to clear the paths." She got out of the cab, and Fergus' excitement ratcheted up. As soon as she released him from the back seat, he shot off into the bushes.

At Caleb's raised eyebrows, Luca said, "Don't worry, he'll be back soon. He just needs to do his patrol."

He spotted a wide-scooped shovel leaning against the cabin wall. "Why don't I do the clearing while you unload?" he offered, glad for a reason to stretch his tense muscles.

"Outhouse is right there." Luca pointed to a sturdy looking shack at the edge of the trees. "If you make a trail to it and to the woodpile that's all we need. When you're done, can you bring in a load of firewood?"

"Will do."

As predicted, it only took a few minutes to get the outside chores done. Once he returned the shovel to its place, Caleb took his phone from his pocket. Not that he didn't trust Luca, but it didn't hurt to check for himself. *Nope. No service.*

Teri had been fine with Caleb being out of touch for a couple of nights. She'd practically pushed him to go, in fact, which he wasn't sure how to take.

Owen, on the other hand, had been jealous. "Can I come, Dad?" he'd pleaded. "I want to go to Luca's cabin, too."

"Maybe next time." Saying the words gave him a shiver of anticipation. It was getting easier and easier to think of Luca being in his life for the long-term. Owen's clear acceptance of her, as well as his own undeniable attraction, were proving hard to ignore.

Defiantly, he turned off his phone. It was useless anyway, but the action felt like stepping off a diving board—irrevocable and stomach-churning.

Fergus returned from his wanderings and kept Caleb company as he stacked as much split wood as he could carry on one arm. Thankfully, there appeared to be enough to last for days and he wouldn't have to reveal his woeful incompetence with an axe. Balancing his load carefully, he opened the door.

Fergus bolted past, almost tripping him up, and headed straight for his water bowl. Enthusiastic lapping sounds ensued.

Caleb followed more sedately and was greeted by the comforting warmth of a wood fire and the spicy scent of chili. His stomach growled. "That smells awesome. Where do you want this?" he said, securing the stacked logs with a hand on top as he toed off his boots.

Luca looked up from the pot she was stirring. "Box next to the fireplace."

It wasn't actually a fireplace but a wood burning stove, set in the corner of the room opposite the kitchen. He could feel the heat emanating from the metal as he tumbled the pieces in the box as directed. Brushing the sawdust and bark off his sleeves and gloves, he turned to take his first good look at the cabin.

A couple of lanterns hanging on the walls flickered with golden light, presumably fueled by lamp oil. Luca was working by the light of another placed on the counter. The kitchen was an L-shape along the rear and side wall opposite the door. Blue flames licked the pot she had warming on the stove, and he was surprised to see her open a small fridge and store some of the fresh supplies they'd brought inside, before realizing both were powered by propane, the tank currently out of sight.

Fergus drank his fill and plopped down next to Luca's feet, eyes bright, ears perked. She reached under the counter and came out with a rawhide bone. "Here you go, buddy." Fergus took the treat gently and disappeared through a doorway in the rear wall.

"Make yourself at home," Luca said, smiling at Caleb. "I know it's early, but I'm starving, so I thought we'd eat right away. I put our stuff in the far bedroom, if you need anything from your gear." She gestured in the direction Fergus had gone.

"Thanks." *Our* stuff. *Bedroom* singular. Anticipation, a simmering current all afternoon, threatened to spark into action, but he told himself to be patient. They had two full nights together, and all the hours in between. There was plenty of time.

Experiencing a flush of heat that wasn't entirely because of his nearness to the fire, he unzipped his parka and hung it on one of the hooks near the door. He lowered himself onto the battered couch that faced a wide window, his back to the kitchen. With the lights inside and the darkness out, the glass acted like a mirror, though he could tell it would normally give a wonderful vista over the lake.

"The view's better in the daytime, obviously. We'll explore it up close tomorrow," Luca said, echoing his thoughts. "We've got snowshoes in the back. We'll dig them out and go for a hike."

He watched her reflection. It gave him an odd sense of distance, as if he were studying her through a television screen. She wore a thin turtleneck under a plaid shirt, well-worn jeans, and thick socks, and moved with sure and confident efficiency around the workstation.

His mouth watered, and not for the chili she was preparing.

LUCA WATCHED CALEB watch her from his seat on the couch. Not that he was facing her way, but she could use the window as a mirror just as easily as he could.

It gave her a frisson of power to know he couldn't keep his eyes off her, any more than she could him. They were going to have sex tonight, that was a given. The only question was exactly when.

Screw it, she thought. *I'm done waiting.*

Fergus was curled on the dog bed in her bedroom, lazily gnawing at his bone. She shut the door, then returned to the kitchen and snapped off the flame under the chili. In the reflection of the window, Caleb's eyes widened, but he didn't turn around.

"Don't move," Luca said, her voice throaty. She'd been anticipating this moment almost from the day they'd met. That was long enough, even for someone who enjoyed unwrapping presents with excruciating slowness.

Caleb's neck stiffened, but other than that tiny response he obeyed her command.

Her fingers went to the top button of her flannel shirt. She undid it, and then the next, and then the next, deliberately, slowly. When they were all unfastened, she pulled her arms out and laid it on the counter. She still wore her thermal turtleneck, of course, but there was no way Caleb could mistake her intentions.

She strolled around the end of the couch and stood in front of him.

He dragged his gaze from the window and met her eyes. Her knees shook. His pupils were blown, his irises a thin line of smoky quartz, and a red flush coloured his cheekbones. His chest rose and fell in regular breaths—until she started to undo the fly of her jeans. Then it stopped.

He groaned when she pushed the pants down to reveal the leggings underneath.

"I knew I hated winter," he growled.

"Don't worry," she soothed. "It'll all be off soon."

She straddled him, one knee on either side of his hips, and his hands gripped her waist. The couch was an ancient, wooden-framed futon, and grossly uncomfortable, but the heat from the wood stove hadn't had time to permeate the back rooms yet, and she didn't want to ruin the mood by sliding between icy, damp sheets.

Taking her time, she nipped his lips. First his upper, then the lower. She nibbled her way along his jaw to his earlobe, breathing in the scent of his woodsy cologne. His skin warmed under her lips and a vein throbbed along his neck. The tips of his fingers dug into her flesh but he'd taken her instruction to heart and made no other motion.

She tugged at the hem of his thin wool sweater, only to discover soft cotton beneath it instead of the bare skin she needed to touch. "This is why all those sexy reality shows are set in the tropics," she muttered, leaning back and urging him to sit upright. With a few muffled oaths, she managed to divest him of both layers and finally—*finally*—she could press her palms on *him*, with nothing in between.

CHAPTER FOURTEEN

C aleb's chest hairs tickled between Luca's fingers as she traced an exploratory pattern from his collarbones, down between his pecs, and to his abs. He was fit—she'd known that from her glimpses of his body this morning at the polar bear dip—but not gym-rat ripped.

Thank god for that. The last thing she needed was a man who looked better in a swimsuit than she did.

He hissed when she tattooed a line along the waistband of his jeans with her fingertips. Sliding his hands under her shirt, he said, "Fair's fair," and swooped it up, forcing her to lift her arms over her head. Blinded by the fabric, she could only imagine his shocked expression, but the harsh gasping of his breath told her enough. She arched her torso toward him.

While Caleb had been at his house, packing what he needed, she had spent a few minutes debating which of her many sets of sexy lingerie to bring along. She had also stripped down quickly and changed into a bra and panties in deep purple, the lace almost sheer, the ribbons holding up the scraps of fabric thin and delicate.

From Caleb's panting response, she'd chosen well.

Moist warmth engulfed her nipple and she let out a loud shriek. Caleb had one hand on her lower back, but the other continued to grip her shirt above her head. She was in no way frightened, and the soft, smothering darkness and intoxicating helplessness enhanced her pleasure.

He licked his way to her other nipple, the faint scruff of his whiskers abrasive yet arousing. She couldn't control the encouraging, mewling sounds that escaped her, drawn out by each suck of his mouth, each lap of his tongue, and her hips pulsed against his groin.

She had to taste him. The moment she wriggled her arms, he released her, and she yanked off her shirt. He lifted his dark head from her breast just long enough to let her discard her bra, then swooped back in, his eyes closed as if savouring her flavour, lashes sooty against his cheek. From this angle she could see the threads of silver in the mahogany strands.

A shocking surge of tenderness had her wrapping her arms around his head, holding him close, the passion within her more than lust, more than need.

Crap, she thought dazedly. *I'm falling in love with him.*

Unaware of the earthquake that had just shaken her world, Caleb slid his hands under her leggings and cupped her ass. His fingertips trailed along the narrow swathe of material that circled her hips and dipped between her legs.

That distracted him from her breasts. He stared at her. "Can I see?" he said, as if she'd handed him the moon on a platter.

She nodded, unaccountably bashful, still unable to form words after her blinding insight.

"Stand up." He pushed her gently to her feet and she rested a hand on his shoulder for balance.

He shimmied the leggings to her ankles and tugged her socks off. With heart-aching reverence, he hovered his fingers over the lace of her panties and then slowly slid them down, tossing them away.

She stood naked before him—physically, if not emotionally. She needed to keep her nascent revelation hidden. Pushing aside her unease, she cocked a hip and gave him a sultry look.

"You've unwrapped me," she said. "Now what are you going to do with me?"

CALEB WAS GLAD HE WAS sitting down. Luca standing before him totally naked and completely confident was utterly arousing and would have knocked his feet out from under him.

As much as he wanted to touch her, though, he had to do one thing first.

Get naked before his clothing did him permanent damage.

"Hold that thought," he said. He scrambled to release the fastenings of his jeans, planted his feet on the floor and lifted his hips just enough to shove the denim down. Luca bent over to help him, and he just about came then and there when he caught sight of her ass reflected in the window.

He groaned loudly. Luca hesitated, her hands gripping the bunched fabric at his thighs. She looked over her shoulder, and then back at him, a wicked gleam in her eyes. "Like that, do you?" She circled her hips, bending her knees, keeping her hands planted on his legs. His cock bobbed and jerked and he closed his eyes before he lost all control.

A warm hand wrapped around his erection and he just about launched to the ceiling.

"As much as I'd like to play with this for a while," Luca said, her voice a low murmur in his ear, her breath tickling his neck, "I need you inside me now."

"Condom," he managed to say, his eyes still clenched shut. "Jeans. Back pocket."

"Excellent. I knew you'd be prepared." Luca's purr held a note of amusement.

He risked a look. She was crouched before him, searching his pants, and fished out the foil packet with a whoop of triumph.

A crocheted afghan was draped over the back of the couch. He threw it to the floor, spreading it out with hectic movements. Luca sat back on her heels, her skin glowing in the soft lantern light, the circles of her nipples and the triangle of hair between her legs dark in contrast.

He tossed a couch pillow onto the afghan. "Lie down," he directed as he snatched the condom from her fingers and ripped it open.

Gratifyingly, she hurried to comply, stretching out on the blanket. Instead of using the pillow for her head, as he'd intended, she tucked it under her ass, bending her knees, opening herself for him.

His skin felt too tight, and not just his cock. Passion sparked down every nerve, engorged every blood vessel, set his body aflame. If he didn't touch her soon, he might simply combust, vanish in a puff of smoke and ash.

She raised her arms in an open embrace. "Get over here," she said. "I need you."

He slid off the couch and knelt between her legs. Her hands gripped his biceps as his cock nudged her opening, her fingers strong and insistent, urgent, greedy sounds puffing from her lips. Her hips lifted, welcoming him in.

He thrust, and she let out a joyful, emphatic moan.

She was hot and tight and wet and oh god he couldn't wait any longer and he thrust again and her heels were pressing into his back and her hand was urging him down to lay on top of her and he thrust and thrust and thrust. Luca's high-pitched keening kept rhythm with his movements until, with a loud, desperate wail, she stiffened and shuddered under him. Her legs stretched out fiercely, her inner muscles tightening and tightening, her shout of release and euphoria echoing in his ears.

He threw back his head and drove deep one final time, a guttural growl roaring from his throat. His orgasm ripped through him and he collapsed as if his spine had dissolved.

She *oofed* as his weight compressed her, but her arms wrapped around his shoulders and her ankles hooked into the backs of his knees. He lay there, panting, feeling her heart beating against his like the wings of a bird against its cage.

LUCA DIDN'T USE PROFANITY often, but most of the words darting around her brain after the most intense sex of her life were of the four-letter variety.

If *that* was what she and Caleb could achieve with barely any foreplay, what would it be like if they put their minds to it? And she'd been right about the noise. If there had been other cabins on the lake, she was pretty sure their residents would have heard her easily.

She wasn't sure how long they lay there, Caleb slack and boneless above, the floor hard and unyielding beneath. She knew, more than felt, that she was uncomfortable, but she wasn't ready to lose the sense of connection linking her to this man—either physically or emotionally.

His head was tucked into the curve of her shoulder, his breaths huffing against her neck. Her fingers traced the bumps of his spine and she was intensely aware of where their bodies joined. Usually, she was eager to clean up after a bout of sex. This urge to cuddle was new for her.

Caleb heaved in a deep breath and raised his head, laboriously propping himself up on his hands. For a moment he stared down at her. His mouth opened, then closed. She waited, trying to quell a rising anxiety.

"Be right back," was all he ended up saying. Keeping hold on the condom, he slid out of her body, dropped a kiss on her nose, stood up—and then looked around in confusion.

Interpreting his perplexity, Luca said. "There's a garbage can under the kitchen counter. And water in a pot on the stove. It should still be warm enough to wash with. Towels are in the cupboard next to the fridge."

He disappeared from view, his footsteps vibrating through the floor. She sat up, curling her knees to her chest and wrapping the afghan around her shoulders. Water sloshed, and his footsteps returned. "Here." A small towel appeared before her, steaming with heat.

"Thanks." It was ridiculous to be shy now, but she waited for him to return to the kitchen before using the cloth to wash away the aftermath of their encounter.

If only it was as easy to wash away the knowledge she'd fallen in love with him.

She hadn't been looking for a new relationship. Maybe that's why it had happened—she hadn't guarded herself against it. She'd thought she and Caleb could have some fun, scratch a couple itches, and move on.

She knew his priority was Owen. She knew that was the way it should be, that she could have no expectations of being anywhere near as important to Caleb as his son.

She knew she was in trouble. Deep, deep trouble.

CHAPTER FIFTEEN

Caleb had thought having sex with Luca would clarify his feelings for her.

Instead, all it had done was muddle them further.

Tuesday morning he helped pack the truck and lock the cabin. He opened the rear passenger door and Fergus hopped in, and then he slid onto his own seat and braced himself for the rough ride home.

They hadn't spent the entire time in bed, he defended to his own conscience. Accompanied by Fergus, they had snowshoed around the lake and explored the trails leading up into the hills. They'd luxuriated in the wood-fired hot tub while watching the stars and sipping wine.

They'd talked. And talked some more. About everything and nothing.

They'd made love. Repeatedly. With none of the dimming of attraction he'd expected.

It was time to put things into perspective, and getting back to Owen would do that. He blamed his feelings on Christmas. He'd been mildly depressed, having to spend it alone, and Luca had been a welcome solution to that problem.

He squashed the little voice that said she might be the solution to *a lot* of his problems.

As usual when she was driving, Luca didn't seem to expect any conversation as she negotiated the narrow track leading to the wider but no smoother secondary road. In what felt like a much shorter time than it had on the way out, they were soon on the paved section and nearing the highway. Fergus snored on the back seat, worn out from all his adventures.

Caleb turned on his phone and it began dinging and chiming with notifications. He scrolled through them, glad for a distraction from his swirling thoughts.

The first he saw was a string of missed calls from Teri.

Owen.

Not bothering to check when they'd been sent or if she'd left any voicemails, he dialed her number.

"Is everything okay?" Luca asked. He jerked, so focussed on his racing thoughts he'd almost forgotten where he was.

"No. Teri tried to call me." One ring. Two rings.

"Caleb." Teri's voice was clear and strong. "You must be on your way back," she said with irritating obviousness.

"What's going on?" he asked, terror tightening his throat so he could barely force the words out. "Is Owen okay?"

"Didn't you listen to my messages?"

"We just got back into service. *Is Owen okay?*"

"He's fine. Which you'd know if you hadn't panicked and checked your voice mail."

"Can we discuss my phone etiquette later?" The worst of his alarm receded, but Teri wouldn't have called at all without a good reason. "If Owen's okay, why were you trying to get in touch?

"To tell you he broke his arm, that's all. He was sledding with some other kids and hit a tree."

His fading anxiety shot to the stratosphere. Calamitous visions danced in his head and he swallowed down bile. "*Hit a tree*?" He felt rather than saw Luca shoot a glance his way.

"Not hard, just awkwardly. He tried to stop himself and jammed his arm the wrong way." Teri was a protective, vigilant mother. But as a nurse, her day-to-day experiences with life-threatening crises meant she viewed most injuries and accidents *far* more calmly than Caleb.

"Did he hit his head?"

"I'm telling you, he's *fine*. I brought him to Emerg and they did a thorough check. There is nothing wrong but a broken ulna. He handled the anesthetic like a champ and has been great since I brought him home."

"*Anesthetic*? They had to put him under?" Caleb's horrified exclamation had Luca jerking the pickup to the shoulder and slamming to a stop. Fergus, startled from sleep, leapt to his feet and barked once, short and sharp. Caleb ignored the dog and spared one quick, distracted glance at Luca.

"They needed to realign the bone. Honestly, Caleb, calm down. Maybe it's a good thing you were out of town. You would have sent Owen into a tizzy if he'd seen you reacting like this."

She was right. He drew in a deep breath, let it trickle out slowly. "Sorry. You know me." She did. What she considered his overprotectiveness had been a contentious point between them since Owen's birth. "I'm calm now. When did this happen?"

"Sunday afternoon. A couple hours after you said you were leaving."

About the same time Caleb had been having sex with Luca. His son had needed him, needed his comfort and support, and Caleb had been oblivious and out of reach.

He hadn't known it was possible to hate himself as much as he did right now.

CALEB DISCONNECTED the call, lowered his phone to his thigh, and rubbed his eyes with the heel of his free hand.

"I gather something happened to Owen," Luca said cautiously. She wanted to touch him, offer what comfort she could, but his stiff, wooden posture rejected such an advance. It was as if an invisible forcefield surrounded him, an impassable barrier she didn't dare breach. "But he's okay?" She hated the tentative tone in her question. Owen *had* to be okay. She didn't know how Caleb would survive if—

She wasn't going there, even in her head.

"He broke his arm tobogganing." Caleb stared out the windshield, flipping the thin rectangle of his cell phone over and over on his thigh. She didn't think he was aware he was doing so, his thoughts obviously with his son. "Had to have anesthesia so they could set it."

"A broken arm doesn't sound so bad." It certainly didn't seem to warrant the pale, set expression on Caleb's face. "I broke mine once, when I wasn't much older than Owen is now. He'll be fine."

"It doesn't matter that he'll be fine. What matters is that he needed me and I wasn't there. I was having a smutty weekend with a near stranger when my son was in *surgery*."

She recoiled, his bitter tone and caustic words a physical blow. His view of their time together was so at odds with her own, it was as if she'd dropped into an alternate dimension. Her cheeks buzzed and she gripped the steering wheel, dizzy and sick to her stomach.

"Can we get going?" Caleb said brusquely. He hadn't looked directly at her since his call to Teri. "I need to see Owen. I should have been with him two days ago. The least I can do now is get there as quickly as possible."

"Of course." Her lips felt numb. She put the truck in gear with deliberate motions, as if any sudden gesture might shatter her. She shoulder-checked and pulled back onto the road.

When she looked back on the next forty-five minutes, she couldn't remember any details of the drive. Her brain was on autopilot as she sped into town and followed Caleb's terse directions to Teri's house. She was still grappling with the cruelty of his comments, stunned at his sour hatefulness regarding what she thought had been a life-affirming, life-*changing* forty-eight hours.

She hadn't misread him that badly, had she? Before they'd left the cabin, she'd been basking in a sense of joy and completeness, glowing from his sensitive, sensuous attention and intimate, affectionate conversation.

Smutty weekend? Near stranger?

He directed her to park in front of a large modern home. Inflatable Christmas displays lay limp and deflated on the front lawn.

She knew how they felt.

"Should I wait?" she asked uncertainly. She dared not suggest she go inside, not given Caleb's currently frozen expression, though she would have felt better if she could see Owen for herself. The little man had wormed his way into her heart with an ease that hadn't worried her until now.

Until she realized that, if his father rejected her, she'd have little chance of seeing the son again.

"No. I'll get a ride home." He slid out of the cab, opened the rear passenger door, and dragged out his duffel bag. "Goodbye, Luca," he said, still without meeting her eyes.

He strode up the path, knocked on the front door, and entered without waiting for anyone to greet him.

All without a backward glance at the devastation he'd left behind.

CHAPTER SIXTEEN

Teri reluctantly allowed Caleb to stay for lunch, rather begrudgingly extending the invitation into the afternoon when he ignored her hints to leave. He needed to reassure himself Owen truly was okay, even though his son had shown absolutely no trauma or distress from the moment Caleb had arrived.

Finally, around four o'clock, he capitulated to Teri's repeated suggestions she drive him home, and the three of them made the short journey to the duplex. Teri pulled into the driveway, parking behind Caleb's car, but didn't turn off the engine.

Owen piped up from his place in the back seat. "Can I show Luca my cast?" He was busting with pride at the bright pink plaster encasing his right forearm and had insisted Caleb sign it the instant he'd walked in the door this morning.

He felt a clutch of guilt at the mention of Luca. He'd said unforgivable things in his panic. Again. "Maybe another time, buddy. I think your mom wants to get home."

Teri and Owen still lived in the house Caleb and Teri had bought as newlyweds. The house where they had brought Owen home, a tiny, wizened creature with a fierce scowl. The house where he'd taken his first steps, said his first words, lost his first tooth.

Looking at the duplex now, though, Caleb realized *this* was home. Until this moment, it had just been a place to live, a necessary evil since he and Teri could no longer reside in the same space.

The last month, though, memories had been made within its walls that made it more than just shelter.

Memories created by and with Luca.

"I'll be quick," Owen said, fidgeting with the strap of his seatbelt. "Please, Mom?"

"Not today, Owen," Caleb said before Teri had a chance to reply. Luca's side of the duplex was dark, the curtains drawn tightly and the porch light off. Even the Christmas lights around the front window were dull and lifeless. "It doesn't look like she's home, anyway."

"Her car's here." Persistence might be a virtue in many situations, but right now, Caleb wished his son had a little less of it.

"You'll be back in a couple days, and your cast doesn't come off for weeks. You'll have plenty of other chances to get Luca to sign it."

Even if she never talked to Caleb again—a fate he uncomfortably realized might be what he deserved—he *knew* she wouldn't take it out on Owen. And if the only way to show he regretted his words and actions was to let his son keep Luca as a friend, then that's what he'd do.

But that didn't mean he couldn't try and repair the damage he'd done.

LUCA FELT LIKE A SPY in a bad movie. She'd been alerted to the vehicle pulling into Caleb's driveway by Fergus and scurried to her current position at the edge of the window in her darkened living room. She peered through the tiny gap between the curtain and the glass and studied the van parked behind Caleb's car.

After swapping her father's truck for her little green machine, she had returned home, still lost in the deep sense of disconnect swamping her. She'd unpacked the items she'd brought back from the cabin, taken a long, hot shower, pulled on comfy clothes, and then curled up on the couch with Fergus. She'd thought about turning on her Christmas lights, but felt they'd only mock her grim mood. But the lack of lights only made the small Charlie Brown tree she'd set up a few weeks ago, already well past its prime and shedding needles, an even more dismal symbol of her dejection and regret.

She had ignored it and found something to binge-watch on Netflix for the afternoon. *Something* being the operative word. She didn't remember a single detail about the sitcom she'd chosen.

Caleb's words had stripped her of any illusions she might have held regarding him, any dreams she might have been building for the future. Yet the entire time she'd tried to lose herself in the fictional screen world, she'd been listening for his return. She didn't want to talk to him, but she wanted to know he was near, wanted to imagine him moving about his home, separated from her only by drywall, lumber, and paint.

The driver hadn't turned off the engine. Luca could make out two figures in the front, and then the flash of something colourful in the back seat. When the passenger door opened,

121

triggering the interior light, she confirmed it was Caleb, and felt safe assuming the dark-haired woman in the driver's seat was Teri. Owen sat in the back, his face animated and cheerful, and she breathed a sigh of relief.

Caleb shut the door, went to the rear of the vehicle, and opened the hatch. Retrieving his bag, he shut the back, waved to Owen through the window and made his way to his front door, without a single glance in the direction of Luca's house.

She'd thought she'd been hurt when Trent refused to put her before his career.

It was nothing compared to the pain of being pushed aside by Caleb.

The worst part was, she couldn't blame him. Maybe that's why the ache was so searing, so destructive. He was a father. He *had* to put his son first. If he didn't, he wouldn't be the man she thought he was, and she wouldn't have been able to love him as she did.

But loving him meant he could hurt her.

And, boy, did she hurt.

CALEB SPENT A RESTLESS, sleepless night and knew he deserved every gritty, grueling minute of it. Even Waldo was treating him with disdain—though that was more likely his response to being deserted for two days than anything to do with Luca.

Caleb *knew* he'd been a total jerk, and the more he relived what he'd said and done, the deeper his guilt grew. In his pointless panic, he'd lashed out at a woman who'd been nothing but caring to both himself and his son. It hadn't been her fault Owen had broken his arm. Sure, the timing had been unfortunate, with Caleb out of reach, but his reaction had been all out of proportion to the situation.

Once he'd been able to think calmly, he remembered that Teri had had the means to get in touch if she'd thought Owen really needed him. She had Luca's father's phone number—at Luca's suggestion, he remembered with a wince—and if something truly drastic had happened, he had promised to get Caleb immediately.

God, he had *really* screwed up.

By eight o'clock the morning after their return from the cabin, Caleb could barely move under the crushing weight of his regret. He lay in bed, staring at the ceiling as he had for much of the night, excruciatingly aware of Luca on the other side of the wall behind his head. Each side of the duplex was a mirror image of the other, so he knew her bedroom was next to his. So close, and yet so far.

It was time to man up and apologize.

Determined not to delay any longer, he rolled out of bed and into the shower. He shaved with special attention, and even took time to put product in his hair and style it properly. He wanted Luca to know his intentions were serious, that he realized how brutish he'd been, and that he was resolved to make it up to her.

CHAPTER SEVENTEEN

T wenty-four hours of wallowing in self-pity was enough. Just because she felt like doing nothing but curling up on the couch and eating junk food—for the second day in a row—didn't mean she should.

Luca was done moping. She'd survived the breakup of an eight-year relationship. She could survive this.

"When in doubt, get outdoors," she told Fergus with forced cheerfulness. "Come on, boy, let's go for a hike." At the moment, her feet felt embedded in concrete and her heart carved from stone. Every action dug deep into her reserves of energy, but she refused to give in to inertia.

In defiance of her gloomy mood, the weather was a perfect winter day. The sun shone from a clear blue sky and the temperature, though crisp and cold, was bearable. She bundled herself in appropriate gear, including a small backpack with a couple bottles of water and snacks for both herself and Fergus. Several hours in the woods would improve her attitude.

She hoped.

Clipping Fergus' leash to his harness, she led him out the back door and around to the side gate. Making sure it shut behind them, she rounded the corner of the house and came to a sudden stop.

Caleb was on the front step, hand raised to knock, staring at her over his shoulder.

She really had to stop meeting ex-lovers this way.

"Luca," he said, lowering his hand and turning to face her.

"Caleb." Feeling at a disadvantage while he was several feet above her on the stoop, she lifted her chin in defiance.

Fergus barked, tail wagging gleefully, tugging hard on his leash in an effort to get to Caleb. The two had formed a strong bond while at the cabin, and she tried not to let Fergus' joy feel like a betrayal.

"I came to apologize." Caleb fidgeted with the narrow white envelope he held in his hands, spinning it between his fingertips. Recalling Owen's sweet, laboriously printed invitations, Luca felt a jolt of sadness.

He was waiting for her response. "No need," she said, concentrating on keeping her pain out of her voice. "You were worried about Owen."

"There *is* a need." He descended the stairs and she took an involuntary step back, but was prevented from going too far when Fergus lunged forward again. Caleb must have noticed her flinch, though, as he stayed near the steps and didn't come closer.

He crouched slightly to pet Fergus' head, but his gaze never left her face. "There *is* a need," he repeated. "I said unjustifiable things. Deplorable things."

She didn't have to be reminded. The *smutty weekend* comment had hurt, but not a fraction as much as labelling her a *near stranger*. Mind you, neither judgment had made her feel good about herself.

"You're right," she said. "You *do* need to apologize. But if you're only doing it to make yourself feel better, don't bother. If you really think we were just two strangers having sex, I don't want to hear it."

His eyes closed briefly. "We weren't. We *aren't.*"

A spark of hope flickered in Luca's soul. She ruthlessly suppressed it. "Are you sure? You basically blamed me for Owen's accident. Would a friend do that? Would a lover?"

"You may have noticed, but I'm not always rational when it comes to my son." A wry smile quirked Caleb's mouth, and that self-deprecating gesture made her furious. What right did he to make her feel tender and forgiving with just one tiny expression? He'd been a jerk, and he deserved her rage. She gripped Fergus' leash tighter, tamping down the urge to shout and scream her hurt and anger, unwilling to make a scene in full view of any prying neighbours.

"Owen had a hard time with our divorce," Caleb went on, "and I promised I would always be there for him, no matter what the circumstances. And then I wasn't."

"Because you were with me." Luca nodded. "Here's the thing. I played second fiddle to Trent's career for a long time. I made myself change to be the woman he said he wanted. When he blamed me for things that weren't my fault, I didn't argue, just accepted it as my due. I hated what I became when I was with him, and when I left, I vowed I would never tolerate someone who made me feel that way, ever again."

"Luca..." Caleb's arm stretched out, hand palm up, open and vulnerable.

She stepped back again, dragging a protesting Fergus with her. Over his whines, she said, "I understand you'll never be able to put me ahead of Owen," she said. "I'm not asking you to. But I also won't allow myself to be unappreciated. To be thought of as *less* because of who I am or what I do."

"What are you saying?"

She shook her head, not sure what she was denying. "I don't think it's going to work between us, Caleb."

THIS WASN'T GOING *at all* the way Caleb had envisioned it.

Not that he'd expected Luca to forgive him easily. He didn't deserve that. But he had never dreamed she wouldn't accept his apology, wouldn't give him a second chance.

Wouldn't fall in love with him, like he had with her.

Suddenly, he needed the support of the railing edging Luca's stoop. His knees shook, his gut fluttered. He loved Luca Tannon. How could that be? They hadn't known each other a month.

His head needed time to get used to the idea, but his heart knew it was the truth. He was in love with Luca, and he'd already ruined things.

She stood before him, dressed in a puffy parka and knee-high winter boots, wearing a knitted toque, heavy mittens, and a bulky scarf, Fergus panting at her side. Her eyes, always warm and welcoming and gleaming with an inner joy, were flat and cold.

His heart seized and he scrambled to regain his mental balance. He'd deal with his own emotions later. Right now, he had to keep Luca from shutting him out of her life for good.

"I appreciate you, Luca. I think you're amazing. But Owen is my son. He has to come first," he said, desperate to explain, but not sure how to go about it.

"I know. I understand."

She didn't, though. How could she, when she didn't have a child of her own? "I can't possibly choose you over Owen," he said. But the thought of losing Luca sliced his soul like a million paper cuts.

"I'm not asking you to!" she said on an exaggerated huff of air. "One of the things I like best about you is how much you love Owen, how much work you put into being a good father. I don't have to be a parent to understand your child's welfare has to be your priority." Her eyes closed briefly and her lips pressed together. "That's why we have to end whatever this is between us. It's not fair to Owen, and it's not fair to me."

There was something terribly wrong with Luca's reasoning. She seemed to believe everyone in his life needed to be slotted into neat little rankings. Love was more fluid than that, and while balancing everyone's concerns could be difficult in any family, Caleb was certain Luca would bring more to his life than she would take away.

There had to be a solution, but he was in too much turmoil to figure it out. Suddenly aware of the envelope in his hands, he shoved it into his pocket. He'd thought she might think it sweet if he wrote out his apology, mimicking the early days of their friendship when letters had passed back and forth between them.

That gesture seemed rather pathetic now, given the revelation that had just burst upon him and her explanation of her own feelings. He needed to regroup, rethink, reorganize.

"Can we talk about this later?" he said. "I don't want to lose what we have, what we *could* have, because I said some stupid, thoughtless things. I'm sure there's a way to fix this."

She scrutinized his face. He wondered what she was searching for and his pulse thundered in panic.

"I don't think there is," she said finally, her shoulders slumping on a long sigh. "It's not about what you said. Not anymore. It's about what's best for all of us."

She couldn't possibly believe life was so black and white. "There's room for both of you in my life."

"I don't want to be the person you *make room* for," Luca said. "I want to be the person that lights you up from the inside. The person you need as much as you need Owen." She flipped her wrist in a dismissive gesture that asked him to step out of her way. He stumbled onto the lowest tread of the steps leading to her door. "Fergus needs his walk. Say goodbye to Owen for me, will you?" With determined strides, she led Fergus to her car, let him into the back, slid onto the driver's seat, and drove away.

CHAPTER EIGHTEEN

For god's sake, Luca thought, *now what?*

Trent stood on her front step, watching her pull into the driveway.

She really didn't have the resources to deal with him now, not after ending it with Caleb this morning. Even a long, brisk hike in the winter woods had done little to settle her emotions.

She'd thought she'd feel better by making a clean break with Caleb. Instead, she had the feeling she'd taken the coward's way out. Instead of accepting her place in Caleb's life and trying to build on what he was able to give, she'd run scared.

And now she had to face the reason *why* she'd run. Or rather, the *who*.

With deep reluctance, she climbed out of her car, flipped the seat forward so Fergus could jump out of the back, and went to meet Trent.

"Where have you been?" he said in way of greeting, for all the world as if he'd told her he was coming and she was late.

"What are you doing here?" she countered. "I've said all I have to say to you." *More than once.*

His aggrieved expression softened, but she sensed it was more a tactic than a true change in emotion. "Let me in, Luca. I just want to talk."

She stepped past him and unlocked the front door. Fergus bounded in, heading straight for his water bowl in the kitchen. Trent took her silence for consent and followed her, shutting the door behind him.

"Don't bother taking off your coat," she said when he reached for the zip of his jacket. "You're not staying."

"Fine." He still undid the fastening, but didn't remove it. "I'm going to be honest with you, Luca. I need you back. Letting you go was a big mistake."

Letting her go was a mistake? He hadn't *let* her go. She had left. "Why?" she said, morbidly curious to see what he might come up with.

His eyes widened. "What do you mean?"

"Why was it a mistake? Do you love me so much you can't live without me?" His mouth opened and closed and she had her answer. "You know what, Trent? You don't miss *me.* You miss the convenience of a ready-made date, someone to drag out when you need her and then tuck away when you don't."

"That's not it at all." A flush streaked the skin of his neck.

"It's not? Then what is it? Tell me straight out."

Again, he couldn't answer her pointed question.

"At least you're not lying to me," she said with a sigh. "I'm sorry if things aren't working out the way you want them to, Trent. Welcome to the real world."

For the first time in a long, long time, Trent dropped his brittle, shiny exterior and looked at her with an expression that revealed his inner confusion. When they'd met, she'd believed it was a measure of the depth of their relationship that he presented such a different face to her than to anyone else. But over the years that openness had come less and less frequently, until she couldn't remember what that man had been like.

"The real world sucks," Trent said, his voice ringing with a sincerity she hadn't heard from him in years.

It struck her that Caleb had never hidden from her. He was the same person with Owen, even strangers, as he was with her. She'd seen him angry, joyful, frightened, and affectionate, and not realized until this moment that the one thing he'd *always* been with her was *honest*. He had hurt her, but he didn't play the games that seemed to come instinctively to Trent.

"I did love you once," she said. "I got tired of competing with your job for slivers of your time." It was pointless to explain how she'd felt like a marionette he manoeuvred at will, one he could dress as he liked, make speak as he wanted. He thought he'd been helping her become someone better, not crushing the person she was.

It was a day for revelations, as another one struck on the heels of her first. Other than one thoughtless remark said in the throes of an anxious moment, Caleb had never made her feel like she wasn't worthy of his attention. He'd never ignored her or pushed her aside. When she'd been with him and Owen, she'd felt one of their team, not an outsider.

Maybe she needed to look at the three of them as equal parts of a whole, not rungs on a ladder.

CALEB WAS BEGINNING to think he had latent stalker tendencies. He found himself constantly drawn to monitoring Luca's movements. The dividing wall between their homes was strong and thick for fire protection, and he could rarely hear more than Fergus' occasional bark. He was reduced to staring out the front window more often than rationality dictated.

Which was why he was aware of Trent's visit the same day she'd ended their relationship, and that she had gone grocery shopping the next afternoon. Each time he'd checked today, her car had been in its accustomed place. But when Teri dropped Owen off as scheduled at three o'clock, it was gone. Somehow, she'd slipped away during one of the few times he'd left his post.

He was standing at the window again—her parking spot still empty—when Owen popped up next to him, Waldo draped over his pink-casted arm. "Can we make the blanket fort now," he said, "so we're ready for later? When is Luca coming over? You invited her, right, like I asked?"

Caleb had promised Owen he could stay up until midnight to ring in the new year, and that they'd pass the time until then playing games and watching movies. Which required the construction of yet another blanket tent, of course. While Caleb had his doubts his son would make it much past ten o'clock, that didn't matter.

What did matter was that he was going to be disappointed at Luca's non-appearance.

"I'm sorry, buddy," he said, crouching so they were eye to eye. "Luca's a little mad at me right now, and I don't think she'd want to come over."

"Did you even invite her?"

Caleb shook his head, feeling the world's worst coward.

"Then how do you know she won't? Maybe she's not mad anymore."

"I'm pretty sure she is. I hurt her feelings pretty bad." *Mad* was probably the wrong word to describe Luca. She had been furious—he'd seen it in her eyes. But she'd also been disappointed, he realized now. Much like his son at the moment.

If he was serious about getting Luca back into his life, it was time to have a serious conversation with Owen.

"Hey, buddy. Let's sit for a minute." He lowered himself to the couch and patted the cushion next to him. Owen let Waldo jump out of his arms and then climbed up beside Caleb.

How do I begin? he thought, then decided to start off easy.

"You like Luca, right?" he said.

Owen nodded vigorously. "Yes. She's fun. And I like Fergus."

"I like them both, too." He took a deep breath. "I know you were really upset when your mom and I decided to get a divorce."

Owen lowered his gaze. "Yeah, but it's okay now."

"You've been very brave, and I'm proud of you." He smoothed Owen's hair and encouraged him to look up. "You remember how your mom and I explained it had nothing to do with you? How it was just that, sometimes, two grownups can't get along, and they shouldn't live with each other anymore?"

His son nodded.

What was the best way to explain the complexities of adult relationships to an eight-year-old? Especially when he didn't quite understand them himself. Carefully, Caleb said, "The thing is, just because I don't want to live with your mom, doesn't mean I want to be alone all the time."

Owen tilted his head. "I worry about that when I'm at Mom's house. That's why I wanted to get Waldo. So you wouldn't be lonely when I'm not here."

Emotion burned the back of Caleb's throat. "I didn't know that. Thank you." Giving into the urge, he dragged Owen onto his lap. He was getting too big for cuddles, but today he snuggled in just like he had as a toddler. Caleb blinked back tears and kept his voice light. "What if I spent more time with Luca? Would you be okay if she was my friend, and I saw her when you weren't around?"

"Like when you went to the cabin with her?"

Caleb's mind tumbled with images of the things he and Luca had done together. And not just the sex. The companionship, too. "Yes. Something like that."

He felt Owen's nod. "I think that would be a good idea. I wouldn't worry about you as much, then."

"I can't guarantee anything," Caleb warned. "She might not want to be my friend anymore. But I want to try, and I wanted to make sure you were okay with it, first."

Owen sat up, twisting on Caleb's lap so he could look him in the face. "Did you say you were sorry? You always make me apologize when I hurt someone's feelings."

"I did. She was still upset."

"Then you didn't do it right. If you'd done it right, she'd forgive you. I don't want her to be mad at us."

"She's not mad at *you*," Caleb replied automatically, his thoughts catching on Owen's words. Maybe he *hadn't* done it right. He'd apologized for his words, and Luca had said she'd forgiven him. What he hadn't apologized for was how he'd made her *feel*. He'd been caught in an endless cycle of useless thoughts the last couple of days, trying to find the right way to explain how important she was to him, as important as Owen even if in a different way. Maybe what he had to do was *show* her. Show her how much he valued her.

How much he loved her.

"I might need your help, Owen," he said. "Let's get Luca back."

CHAPTER NINETEEN

Luca was not a big fan of New Year's Eve in general. She'd had her fill of loud, raucous parties, and thought it ludicrous anyone believe that an arbitrarily decided changing of a date could alter your life.

That she was feeling particularly cynical this year had nothing to do with the man living next door, she told herself. Repeatedly.

The thought of staying home alone, however, held few attractions, especially since she knew the aforementioned man would be home as well, enjoying time with his son. So when Niki called to invite her to a small gathering she and Danielle were hosting, Luca had agreed.

She even offered to go over early and help her sister and fiancée prepare for the rest of their guests. Owen was going to be dropped off at Caleb's at three o'clock, and Luca didn't want to be around when that happened, for too many reasons.

Spending the evening with a group of lively, intelligent people had been better than being alone. She'd even had fun playing Cards Against Humanity and counting down to midnight with the small group Niki and Danielle had collected. But when she'd returned to her dim and dark home around one a.m., the loneliness she'd been denying came crashing down.

She couldn't ignore the feeling she'd made a huge mistake shoving Caleb away. Her insistence that his love had to be split into fragments seemed naive and petty. When she thought about how she felt for Caleb and Owen, she realized her love was big enough to encompass both, without a need to rank one above the other. Could she trust Caleb to feel the same?

It took her a long time to fall asleep, with the result she lay in bed much later than usual on New Year's Day and probably would have stayed under the covers even longer if Fergus hadn't demanded to be let out. Bleary-eyed, she dragged herself down the hall to the kitchen and let him into the back yard, then went to make herself a large pot of coffee.

The glimpse she'd gotten when she'd opened the door for Fergus had shown her snow falling, light by steady, from a dull silver sky. A cold front was moving north, precipitation trailing behind it. Luca foresaw copious amounts of shovelling in her future. Maybe the exertion would help her sleep.

She wasn't sure how long Fergus had been barking when she finally grew conscious of it. He often greeted the neighbourhood squirrel and birds in the mornings, but there was something different about his yelps today. Rubbing the heels of her hands into her eyes to wipe the last of her drowsiness away, she looked out the window.

A large figure was perched on the long branch overhanging her yard from the tree in Caleb's yard.

She blinked. It was still there.

Caleb's legs dangled, his heavy winter boots swinging back and forth. He gripped the branch above his head with one hand, while the other was braced against the limb near his hip.

Below him, Fergus was dancing and barking, delighted at this new game.

What on *earth* was going on?

CALEB BALANCED UNCOMFORTABLY on the branch and watched Luca's kitchen window. If this didn't work, he was going to feel more of a fool than he already did. Snow fell thick and fat, creating a veil between the tree and her house, but he could see her silhouetted against the glass. Then she disappeared.

All he could do now was wait.

Fergus had started barking the moment Caleb inched his way out on the thick limb and hadn't stopped. He peered down between his dangling feet. "Hey, boy," he called. "It's just me. Give it a rest, will you?" The last thing he wanted was to have other neighbours come to investigate what the fuss was about and discover him swinging here.

Caleb and Owen had planned their campaign carefully, but the potential for embarrassment was great.

The first step had been keeping close watch for Fergus to make an appearance in the back yard. They both knew that would be a sign that Luca was awake. That had necessitated frequent glances out the back door, as there wasn't a good view from any window. Thank goodness the weather had warmed up and peeking outside didn't mean risking hypothermia. Caleb and Owen took turns starting at seven in the morning, and were finally rewarded for their patience shortly after eight.

"Quick, Dad!" Owen shouted. "He's out! Fergus is out. You've got to get in the tree!"

It was Owen that had suggested Caleb climb the tree to get Luca's attention. At first, Caleb had scoffed. "I was thinking of inviting her to dinner. Maybe giving her a small piece of jewellery or big bouquet of flowers."

Owen had shaken his head solemnly. "You hurt her feelings, Dad. You have to do something extra special so she won't be mad anymore. Remember how worried she was when I went after Waldo? If you make her worry about you, she'll *have* to forgive you."

Caleb didn't bother pointing out that, if Luca was mad enough, she'd be only too happy to see Caleb in danger. In the end, he had agreed to Owen's plot. After all, his own efforts to fix things had fallen flat and he was desperate enough to take any suggestions he could, even if they came from the brain of an eight-year-old boy. Maybe if he could make Luca laugh, that would be the first step to reconciling their relationship.

As soon as Owen sounded the alert, Caleb had stomped into his boots and dragged on his parka, taken a second to zip Owen's coat closed with his casted arm tucked inside, and then the two of them had raced through the falling snow to the tree in the far corner of the yard. Caleb had already created a secure platform for Owen next to the fence so he could see what was happening on the other side. He lifted him up, made sure he was safe, and then clambered up the tree and along the branch.

Where he was now sitting.

Still waiting for Luca to come to him.

The longer he waited, the lower his heart sunk.

"Is she coming, Dad?" Owen said, hidden behind the fence. His part in the proceedings was to wait until Luca came to see what was going on and then jump up and surprise her. Caleb wasn't sure what that was meant to do, but he had only slim hope the whole escapade would work at all, so what did it matter?

"Not yet," Caleb replied. *Please*, he thought. *Please come out, Luca.*

CHAPTER TWENTY

Caleb was too far away for eye contact, but that hadn't stopped Luca from stepping back from the window hurriedly, her heart pounding.

What the hell was Caleb doing sitting in a tree?

Cautiously she peered around the cabinets framing the window, just far enough to make sure she hadn't gone crazy.

Nope. There he was. Fergus was no longer barking, but still paced under the branch, ears perked, tail wagging.

This had to mean something. Since she'd broken off their relationship, Caleb had made no attempt whatsoever to get in touch. Unless *he* was the one who had gone crazy, this had to be a stunt to get her attention.

And that must mean he wasn't willing to accept her pronouncement it was over. He must want her to give him another chance. To give *them* another chance.

She wondered if she was brave enough to accept his overture.

Hugging her thoughts about the boundless capacity of love tightly, she pulled on her boots with grim determination. Sliding her arms into her coat, she wrapped a scarf around her neck and tugged on a toque. When she could delay no longer, she opened the back door.

Fergus heard her and dashed to her side, then halfway back to the tree, then to her again, saying unmistakably in doggie language, "Come see, come see, you have to come see what I found!" She followed him at a much slower pace, her gaze glued to Caleb. He watched her steadily, his posture relaxed, as if he spent every morning perched in a tree like the world's biggest squirrel.

She came to a stop far enough away that she didn't have to crane her neck and blinked at him through the falling snow. She knew she should say something, but what did you say to the man you'd rejected who was now sitting nonchalantly *in a tree*?

"Is she there, Dad? Has Luca come out yet?" Owen's light, youthful voice, sounding unexpectedly from an invisible source, gave her a start.

"Yes, she's here." Caleb's voice, on the other hand, settled over her like warm honey.

"Hi, Luca!" Owen's head popped up, his chin barely clearing the top of the fence, his cheeks rosy with cold. "Dad and I are surprising you!"

She nodded and found her voice. "You sure are. What's going on?"

"Dad hurt your feelings," Owen explained, "so he needs to apologize."

"I think I've got this, Owen," Caleb said, not taking his eyes off Luca. She could feel his stare right to the tips of her toes. "Thanks for all your help. Why don't you go back inside while I talk with Luca?"

"Make sure you do it right this time, Dad," Owen ordered, and Luca choked off a chuckle.

"I'll try. Careful getting off the bench."

"Daa-aad." Luca wasn't sure if the put-upon tone was in response to Caleb's request to be cautious or to express Owen's doubt at his father's ability to apologize correctly.

"Oww-enn." Caleb matched his son's tone. "Go inside."

With a hefty sigh, Owen disappeared from view. Luca looked over her shoulder and watched him climb the steps to the back door and close it behind him. Taking a deep breath, she turned back to Caleb.

"You already apologized," she said, squinting up through the fluffy flakes. "It might be my turn now. I'm the one that pushed you away."

"I'm the one that made you think that was the only option." He wriggled forward on the branch. "Watch out."

She leaned back on one foot as Caleb dropped out of the tree, landing with bent knees and a slight *oof* less than a metre in front of her.

"What was all that about?" She waved at the leafless branches.

"Owen decided that since you worried about him when he was in the tree, you'd worry about me, too. I don't normally take relationship advice from a child, but since I couldn't come up with anything better, I figured I had nothing to lose."

"I see." What she saw was a man willing to do things outside his comfort zone in order to get her attention. She saw a man who knew her well enough to realize she wouldn't be able to resist such a gesture.

And she saw a man she could trust to find a place for her in his life.

"I was wrong when I said I didn't want you to choose between me and Owen," she said. His expression went blank, and she hastened to explain. "I was wrong because you don't have to. If I have enough space in my heart for both of you, then maybe you have enough space for me, too."

His eyes heated and he took a step forward. Winter air swirled between them, but she felt his warmth and wondered how it was possible the snowflakes could keep falling. Why weren't they melting, like her bones were?

"I can't promise to never hurt you again," he said quietly. "I've got a temper and I say things I shouldn't. But I can promise to try and do better. And I can definitely promise to say I'm sorry when I need to."

"I can live with that." *What I can't live* without *is you.* She wasn't quite ready to say that aloud, though.

RELIEF AND JOY AND a trembling tenderness swelled Caleb's heart. *She's giving me another chance,* he thought dizzily.

"Love's elastic, Luca," he said. "It doesn't make you choose. It just gets bigger and bigger the more people you include. And while life is all about choices, if you choose to love someone, you'll find a way to make it work."

"I'm starting to wrap my head around that concept," she said. "I might need a reminder once in a while, though."

"This kind of a reminder?" Caleb said, stepping forward, wrapping his arms around her, and lowering his mouth to hers.

Luca's lips were chilly, the tip of her nose cold against his cheek. But she opened eagerly under him, and the warmth of their breath mingled, steaming around them.

"I love you, Luca," he said, and her hands, which had been squeezing his biceps, tightened almost painfully. He lifted his head and rubbed his nose against hers. "I wasn't going to tell you. Not so soon, anyway. But if we're going to make this work between us, we need to be honest. I think I've loved you from the moment you made me jump into a frozen lake. Maybe even before. And if hearing me say it will help you trust me again, then why would I keep it a secret any longer?"

Her eyes searched his, her hands sliding up his arms to his neck. She hadn't put on mittens and he gasped at her icy touch. "You're freezing." He unzipped his coat so he could tuck her fingers under his arms to warm them.

"I don't feel cold," she said. "You make me all warm and toasty. Oh, and I love you, too."

He groaned and tucked his face into the curve of her neck and shoulder. "You don't have to say it just because I did," he muttered against her skin.

She pinched him on the sensitive skin on his ribs and he squeezed her hands to his sides, squirming. "I'm not. And just so you know, I'm scared to death. We both know that sometimes love isn't enough."

He raised his head and met her wide, anxious gaze. "It will be this time," he said with certainty and watched the fear fade from her expression, to be replaced with joyous determination. "It will be this time."

EPILOGUE

O nce again, Caleb's living room was littered with brightly coloured wrapping paper and discarded packaging. He couldn't believe a year had already passed since last Christmas. If time kept flying by at this rate, he'd be eighty the next time he blinked.

Which was one more reason not to put off what he and Owen had planned any longer.

His son sat in the middle of the chaos, tongue sticking out of his mouth in concentration as he fiddled with pieces of his new Lego set. Next to Caleb, cuddled under his outstretched arm, was Luca. And next to *her* was the furry mass of Fergus and Waldo, now a near-inseparable duo.

Luca tipped her chin up and smiled. "Can you believe we've known each other a year?" she said in an echo of his own thoughts.

He ran his finger along her shoulder, feeling the strap of the black lingerie that had been his private present to her under the flannel of her pajama shirt. He had plans for stripping her out of the lacy bra and panties once Owen was safely asleep later tonight.

"It feels like forever," he said, and was awarded with a sharp jab in his ribs. "In a good way," he protested, laughing and dropping a kiss on her forehead. "In a *very* good way."

Of course, there had been some major adjustments, and not just for the feline and canine members. Caleb still winced when he thought of the first time Luca had scolded Owen. His son had been shocked at the fact his good buddy wouldn't simply let him do whatever he wanted, like any other friend. Which had led to a discussion on Luca's role that had been awkward and uncomfortable for everyone. But it had cleared the air, and Owen had grudgingly become more accepting of Luca's role as an authority figure as time went on.

He and his son had had another conversation about Luca recently. One he hadn't shared with her yet. There were other things he wanted to mention first. For example—

"I've been thinking about moving," Caleb said. "Finding a bigger place in the new year." He felt her stiffen, then relax. He waited.

"I'll miss having you as a neighbour," she said lightly. "It's been pretty convenient."

Luca's fear of rejection still coloured their relationship, but they'd both been working on it—her, by not assuming the worst, and him, by reinforcing his commitment in words and deeds. Which had meant, once in a while, that Owen didn't come first. Some day, his son would be grown and gone. When that happened, Caleb wanted to be sure Luca would still be in his life.

"It has been," he said. "But I need more office space, including a place other than a dingy basement where I can meet clients." His business was doing well, certainly, but that wasn't the main reason he was thinking of the change. He took a deep breath. "I was also wondering if you wanted to move in with me."

LUCA BLINKED. "WHAT was that?"

A faint flush coloured Caleb's cheekbones. "I thought, maybe, you'd like to live with me," he said gruffly, then nodded his head at Owen, still obliviously playing with his gift. "With us."

"I think that would be amazing," she replied. She could feel her cheeks ache with the force of her smile, despite the tiny flutter of disappointment wriggling in her gut.

It was her own fault. She'd obviously misread the signs. She'd thought Caleb was going to propose, not invite her to live with him. It was the next logical step, of course, even though sharing the duplex was almost the same thing, given they were in and out of each other's homes so often.

During the last few weeks, she'd caught him watching her with thoughtful expressions that he had hurriedly hid, and Owen had been acting oddly in her presence, too. Besides, it was Christmas, and December held a special place in their lives, given it was the anniversary of when they'd met.

It was ridiculous that she felt a little deflated now she knew what he'd been thinking. Moving somewhere new was huge. It would be a home they would choose together, a place that would no longer be *his* and *hers* but *theirs*. It was a *great* idea.

She smiled even more determinedly. "I would love to move in with you and Owen," she said, sealing her pledge with a smacking kiss. "When can we start looking?"

The skin around Caleb's eyes crinkled with his smile. "I already have," he said. "I'll show you my shortlist later. But

153

first..." He turned to Owen. "Hey, buddy. Want to get the other gift now?"

Owen's head shot up, toy forgotten. "Really?"

"Really."

Luca watched in confusion as he scrambled through the discarded wrappings and down the hall. Disturbed by his hurried departure, Fergus and Waldo leaped off the couch and chased after him, adding to the pandemonium. A moment later, the three of them returned in a raucous parade.

Owen carried a small gift bag, tissue paper frothing out of the top, in one hand, an envelope in the other. He came to a rushing stop in front of Luca and held out the envelope.

Her heart started to pound.

"Here," he said, practically vibrating with excitement. "Open this first."

She took it with trembling fingers, then looked at Caleb. He nodded encouragingly, but she saw a hint of nervousness in his warm brown eyes.

Sliding her finger under the flap, she pulled out a single sheet of paper. In Owen's scrawling printing, she read:

Will you marry us?

Both Owen and Caleb had signed their names below those four sweet words.

She couldn't speak around the fullness in her throat, but she hoped her two men could see her acceptance in the glow of her face.

Caleb took the bag from Owen and handed it to her. "We love you, Luca," he said. "*I* love you. Will you be my wife?"

For the first time in her life Luca tore through the wrappings without thought or care. Tissue paper went flying, and she used her nails to rip away the gold paper on the small gift she found at the bottom of the bag.

The jeweller's box she revealed was soft blue velvet. She held it in her hand and stared.

"Open it!" Owen said, jumping up and down and flapping his arms excitedly. "I helped Dad pick it out. Open it!"

Inside was a solitaire diamond on a platinum band. It was simple and elegant and exactly right.

Caleb freed it from the case and she held out her left hand. He slipped it on her finger and she gripped his hand tightly. "It's perfect," she said, staring at him. Owen was still chattering and dancing, but Luca had ears and eyes only for Caleb. He leaned forward and pressed a soft kiss on her lips.

"You haven't said yes, yet," he murmured against her mouth.

She threw her arms around his shoulders. "Yes," she said breathlessly. "Of course, yes!"

"Merry Christmas!" Owen shouted, squirming his way between them.

"Merry Christmas," Luca and Caleb said in unison, and in his face, she read the promise of many more happy Christmases to come.

THANK YOU

Thank you for reading *The Promise of Frost*. I hope you enjoyed it!

Reviews and ratings are a great way to help other readers discover new authors. Just a line or two is all that's needed—or simply click the number of stars you think it deserves. I encourage you to post your honest opinion at the retailer where you purchased your copy. Thank you so much!

ABOUT THE AUTHOR

B renda Margriet writes savvy, slow burn, contemporary romances with ordinarily amazing characters. In her own ordinarily amazing life, she had a successful career in radio and television production before deciding to pilfer from her retirement plan to support her writing compulsion.

Readers have called her stories "poignant," "explicit and steamy," "interesting, intriguing and entertaining," and "unlike any romance you've read before" (she assumes the latter was meant in a good way).

Brenda would love to stay in touch. Subscribe to her newsletter and you'll immediately receive a free read, be able to tag along with her dog-walking adventures, find out what she's reading when she should be working, and other randomness...along with all her writing news, of course! Just click here.

You can also join Brenda on social media—she is most active on Facebook and Instagram. And you can always discover more about her and her books on her website, brendamargriet.com.

ALSO BY BRENDA MARGRIET

Mountain Fire

Reserved for You

No Life But This

When Time Falls Still

The Promise of Frost

THE BENDIXON SISTERS SERIES

Allegro Court

Gateway Crescent

Crossroads Corner

TIMELESS SEASONED ROMANCE

After Words

Richly Deserved

SILVERBERRY SEDUCTION SEASONED ROMANCE

Secrets Under the Covers

Loving Between the Lines

Turn the Next Page

Strictly by the Book

Read excerpts and find buy links at www.brendamargriet.com